A Quizard is Born

In the Doll Land of Sha Bebe

by

Mary Lynn Plaisance

Printed by CreateSpace, An Amazon.com Company

Acknowledgement

Dedicated to all of the humans who still believe in magic,
especially my favorite muse Patty -- Whom I lovingly call, Elfina.

To my favorite guru-- Hope – Whom I lovingly call Tweetie
(KNYBEL)

Chonnie and Miriam, Linda and Ellen
(My soul sisters)

Always to the Spirit of Louisiana

I always acknowledge with much love
My husband Teddy, My children
My grandchildren, My great grandchildren.

May the magic that lives in your heart never go away
and may your love for each other continue until after forever.

Mary Lynn Plaisance

The residents and the dolls of the Magical Doll Land of Sha Bebe

At the end of each month the festive -- run of the quilts -- occurs.

Jolie and Beau Waltzing

One road runs through the Doll Land of Sha Bebe

It's called - The Braided Rug Road - and they sing:

The sun has gone down here in Sha Bebe Land
So we waltz along holding hand in hand
All dressed for bed to rest for the night
Guided by the glow of so many firefly lights

As we dance along the braided rug road
For this is the only passage we know
We remember that we can never go wrong
Cause this road leads us back to our sugar shack home

While waltzing along the braided rug road
Waltzing along the braided rug road
Dancing and dancing we all sing this song
While waltzing along the braided rug road.

When all of the dolls are snuggled in bed
Those beautiful sleepy rag doll heads,
Good dreams will come to them all through the night
Cause making humans happy is their main delight

While waltzing along the braided rug road
Waltzing along the braided rug road,
Dancing and dancing we all sing this song
While waltzing along the braided rug road.

It's a Magical Land of Dolls who travel on a magic flying quilt.

They are alive and speak the same language as in human land.

The Residents of the Doll Land of Sha Bebe

Queen Faustina - Rules the Doll Land of Sha Bebe
Wizard Antoine - Married to Queen Faustina
Children -- Twin Quizards
Madame Plume - Pops the dolls to life with her magic wand
her wand is the most powerful
Madame Poulette - Zaps the magic flying quilts with her magic wand
Lucille, Poulette's pet chicken is *never to be put in a gumbo*
Miss Betty Lou - Teaches the dolls good manners and common sense
Marie La Vie - Wise Healer from the swamp lands and a dear friend
Acadia and Olivia, the good Cajun Fairies plus 20 more
Sugar Mill Ladies - 16 women who cook and cater for all of the dolls
The Cajun Angels - 10 Cajun angels watch over the doll land
Jolie and Beau Dolls-100 boys and girls live there for one month
Jacque and Evangeline -- The ghosts who guard Swamp Alley

The Bebe Land Band

Dupre the Cat -- plays the silver tub drum
T-Roux Raccoon - plays the box guitar and the harmonica
Angelina Alligator -- plays the scrub board
Buddy, the Wizard's pet raccoon - singer

The Haunted Island of Ophelia

Dr. Ophelia Amedee -- The Eccentric Witch Doctor
Ophelia's three minion Dwarf sisters
Clotilda, Matilda, and Emelda
Cromwell -- The mummy
Ghost Girl lives in the well

Content

You have now entered The Magical Doll Land of Sha Bebe. A place where no human has ever been before. You're in for a very exciting journey in this fourth book in the series about The Chronicles of Sha Bebe. The magical doll land has experienced three horrible events before this one. In a land where time has no meaning except when it is measured only by the tick-tock of a human clock, can this magical doll land survive another horrible event?

A Quizard is born to newlyweds Queen Faustina and Wizard Antoine in the month of December at 3:33 pm, which is the exact time that the eccentric 'human' witch doctor, Ophelia Amedee, needs the blue light of a Quizard's heart to keep herself alive and beautiful. A magic key is needed to light the blue heart while saying "The Blue Chant", and this must be done within 24 hours after a Quizard is born, or a Quizard is destined to have no magic at all.

Who is this Quizard that is unknown to everyone but Marie La Vie? Will the mad doctor get the rare Quizard from the doll land of Sha Bebe before 3:33 pm? Where is the magic key?

Something has to give, because Dr. Ophelia Amedee is desperate to stay alive for another 50 years, and she will never give up searching for another Quizard. She must have one at any cost.

Another good book by Mary Lynn H. Plaisance to add to your bookshelf from The Chronicles of Sha Bebe.

Wizard Antoine and Queen Faustina

Chapter 1

The Wedding

Like clockwork from the land of humans, Queen Faustina began feeling antsy again. She felt something was going to happen in the doll land of Sha Bebe that she would have no control over, whatsoever. As Queen of the land, she made all of the rules. No one could ever leave the land without the key seal of approval from the Queen. No one was leaving, so why was she feeling this way?

While the residents of the doll land, along with the 100 boys and girls were under the big oak tree decorating for her wedding, the Queen was sitting on her swing in front of her round, blue stone house. She could not get a grip on why she was feeling antsy that something was out of order, but something was definitely *out of order*!

The first time Queen Faustina had this antsy feeling was when Emily desperately needed the help of the Sha Bebe, because she was grieving the death of her father, and the Queen sent Jolie and Beau running, *on foot* mind you, out of the sugar cane field. It was an emergency. This was a first. No dolls ever had to run out of the land unaccompanied by a magic flying quilt.

The second time Queen Faustina had this *feeling* was when Robes Pierre, The Wicked Cajun Fairy, entered the doll land through the invisible dome in whirlwind of soot. No one in the doll land knew what was going on, and Queen Faustina was swooped away by Robes

Pierre and held as a prisoner. Miss Betty Lou who is the school teacher had her mind all distorted by this wicked villain, the 100 dolls fell asleep, Plume and Poulette left the land without the Queen's seal of approval. Creeping vines almost sunk the entire land. Thank goodness Madame Plume knew what to do with Robes Pierre. That was such a disturbing time for everyone.

The third time Queen Faustina had this strange feeling that she could not shake away was when the Ugly Babies from the other side, another dimension, came into the land of Sha Bebe. They came in through a portal and didn't need to break the invisible dome. This time, Marie La Vie had to come to the rescue. Now, she felt this feeling even deeper than before. It was almost as if her antsy feelings were set to human clocks and calendars. About every 50 years or so, something or someone tries to destroy the goodness of the doll land of Sha Bebe.

She mumbled to herself. "Who is it this time? What do they want? It has to be something no good. It's the only time I feel this way. But when? What? I have a wedding being planned. I love my Wizard Antoine. This is a happy event, and we want a little girl after the wedding. A cute little girl who will bring us more joy and ..."

"Faustina!" Madame Plume interrupted her mumblings. "Where do you want to make your entrance under this huge oak tree?" Her voice was a little loud so the Queen could hear her over all of the talking and music going on under the oak tree, and she startled Queen Faustina.

"Oh, ah…. Over there somewhere." She pointed to the sky.

"You want to make an entrance from the sky?" Plume stiffened as she was a little shocked at her answer.

"No, ah, not the sky. Let me think more about that." She rattled her keys. She had a set of keys on a huge key ring that helped her to think.

"Okay, you have five minutes. You and Antoine are not even dressed yet in the clothes I made for you." Plume was a little annoyed. "Five minutes."

"Okay, five minutes. I'll be ready." Faustina went inside to get her key ring to giggle them. The rattle of her keys helped her to have deep thoughts.

Queen Faustina's big, beautiful oak tree filled
with her doorknob key chimes

Everyone in the doll land was busy decorating under the old oak tree for the wedding of Queen Faustina and Wizard Antoine, including the 100 boys and girls. The Bebe Land Band kept them entertained with music. Dupre the Cat played the silver tub drum. T-Roux Raccoon played the box guitar and the harmonica. Angelina

Alligator plays the scrub board and Buddy, the Wizard's pet raccoon, was singing his heart out.

The 16 sugar mill ladies were busy getting the food arranged under the tree in grand style. So many white candles of all different heights adorned the tables, lots of tall vases filled with green ferns filled the yard, white dinner ware on the table trimmed with gold, and her gold silverware that Antoine made for his Queen from the magic in his hands.

Madame Poulette who made the magic flying quilts, made a special Persian rug for the Queen and the Wizard to stand on and say 'I do' in front of the statues of Jacque and Evangeline. The sugar mill ladies, with the help of the boys and girls planted big blooms of gladiolas all around the statues that Antoine had formed with his own two hands.

Antoine had a gentle spirit, but he also had a temper when he saw an injustice, so his dad waited until he was old enough to use the powers he had in his hands. But, Jacque passed away before he could show Antoine. So when Antoine was stuck in a place called Swamp Alley, the ghost of Jacque and his mom Evangeline came to him on a white cloud, and they both guided him out of Swamp Alley. It was then that the ghost of his dad showed him how to shot his magic bolt of lightning from his hands. That lesson in the alley saved Antoine and others, so he formed the statues of his parents under the oak tree in a beautiful alabaster stone in their memory. They were now the ghost of Swamp Alley and without their help, many years ago, Antoine would not be where he is today, or know that he had a sister.

They had written their own vows, and they would say 'I do' at noon.

Madame Plume walked over to the Queen. "You know, as your maid of honor, I am very much honored to make all of the clothes for everyone in the doll land for your special day," she said as she swung around dancing in her pink dress filed with more feathers than she had ever had on any dress before.

"I really love my dress."

The Queen just stared at Madame Plume. She looked like a big, fluffy, pink peacock with all of those feathers, but Queen Faustina didn't tell her anything. She knew how Madame Plume loved her feathers. That's how she got her name. A plume is a French word for a feather.

"I know you're the bride and all, but I'll be holding your long train behind that fluffy white dress that I made for you," she smiled with a twinkle in her eyes, "but, I want to look good too, you know."

She batted her long eye lashes. "It's not every day I find out," she twirled her feathers, "first that I have a brother after all of these years who's a Wizard, and second, that he'll be marrying my best friend, the Queen and ruler of the doll land of Sha Bebe. I never thought I would see the day you would get married. I'm so happy for you."

Madame Plume kept dancing around, her feathers on her dress swinging every which way in the cool December breeze. Everyone was dressed for the wedding in the clothes she made with her magic wand. She knew how to work her fabrics so well with her magic wand. No one could work fabrics like Madame Plume. Her magic wand was the most powerful. After all, her wand POPPED the dolls to life.

"Plume!" Queen Faustina shouted over the voices of many of the dolls talking and decorating. Also The Bebe Land Band was playing music, while some were singing, and everyone was having a grand time preparing for the wedding.

"Did you ever hear the name Ophelia, or did you ever name a doll Ophelia?"

"I can't hear you." Madame Plume yelled back. "Wait, I'll dance back to you." She made her way around all of the boys and girls who were unrolling yards and yards of pink tulle.

She was near the Queen, and she asked again in a softer voice. "Plume, did you ever hear of the name Ophelia? I have that name on my mind, and it's haunting me in a way I can't explain."

"No, I never heard of the name Ophelia," she answered Faustina still twirling her feathered dress around. "I don't remember naming any doll Ophelia, either. Why?"

"You weren't listening to me, Plume. Stop the dancing for a while." When Plume saw the Queen rattling her keys wildly, she knew something was wrong.

"What's the matter, you alright? You want me to call Marie La Vie to help you?"

"No, no." said Faustina. "I'm fine. Just a little bit nervous I guess because of the wedding. I have the name of Ophelia that keeps popping into my head, and I can't get myself together. I'll be okay. Go and help Poulette decorate. I'll be okay." The Queen smiled, but was not in a smiling mood.

Madame Poulette was in charge of decorations, and she took this festive occasion seriously. The stars that surrounded the bottom of her black dress were keeping up with her movements very well. Madame Poulette would be lost without her stars, the same way that Madame Plume would be lost without her feathers. Faustina, Plume, Poulette and Marie La Vie had been close friends since the beginning of time. Miss Betty Lou entered the doll land much later than the rest of the residents. She was a human before she entered the doll land,

and a very good school teacher in New Orleans.

Queen Faustina wished for Miss Betty Lou to enter the doll land and her wish came true, but she could leave if she was not happy. After staying in the doll land for a while, she was amazingly happy and said she vowed never to go back to the hectic life of the humans. She liked being a doll. She was a nervous worry wart and always on the soft, quite side, but his was just her nature. She was an excellent teacher with her students.

The boys and girls were busy with the wedding decorations. They were wrapping the trees full of pink tulle. She had patience with her 100 little kiddos each month. No worries. No anxiety. She adored her job. When Madame Plume made this bunch of 100 dolls, she didn't let any defects pass her watchful eye. No defects in the fabrics at all this time. That happened only a few times, which lead to unruly students, but Madame Plume could mend defects very well with her wand.

All of a sudden, Queen Faustina yelled to Plume, "Pop an archway right over there with your magic wand. I love pink and white silk flowers. Then the boys and girls can flood the archway with those exotic pink flowers we saw at that shop." She smiled but she was looking around the reception area and under the tree branches as if she was looking for someone or something.

"Plume, remember that special magic place on Royal Street where we bumped into that gas lantern pole in the middle of that courtyard? It took us through a portal which then lead us to that place called Lacey Laurel Lane, with all of those special shops. Remember that shop called *Crystal Balls and All?*"

She was still antsy and looking around.

"Yes indeed. I remember that lovely place. And I remember that courtyard. Ah, the courtyard that was behind that hidden house. We'll need to go back and visit that place. Just you and me."

"Yes, we'll have to do that one day," Queen Faustina said with her eyes as spaced out as Madame Plume had ever seen them. Her neck was stretched out as well.

"Faustina, why don't you and Antoine go on your honeymoon there? Oh, that would be so good for the two of you. No one can see you in the city as a doll. They see us as human, and then you can go into the portal and show Antoine how Lacey Laurel Lane looks." Plume got excited. "Take my brother through the portal..." Plume spun around with that big feathered dress on.... "and you can both be magical dolls and humans. You've never seen Antoine as a human yet. How about that?"

"Yea, that sounds good to me." She sat down on the chair at the wedding table.

The Lantern Portal Pole to enter Lacey Laurel Lane

"Well," she sighed a deep sigh, "I sent a few of the Cajun Fairies in the Fairy Boat to that shop. They only went there once; I hope they make it through the portal pole in that courtyard to get into the big iron gate. They have those pretty pink silk flowers there. Those flowers don't die." She was fumbling around with the lace on her dress.

"I like the silk flowers there… in a place where the streets are filled with magical dolls like us… and no one can get in if they don't know where it is… and the streets have no name after you pass that big gate… and the ……." Faustina paused and let out a deep, long sigh.

"Faustina! What is wrong with you? You okay?" Madame Plume was getting worried. She was in a daze since she first saw her in the morning.

"Ah, I'm okay." She said quickly, and forced a smile with a shorter sigh this time. "Antoine and I will make our entrance through the pink silk flower arch, while all of you can stand over on that end of the yard. That should look pretty," Faustina said with not too much enthusiasm. She turned around and walked away, swiftly.

She loved the Wizard so much, and wanted this wedding more than anything she had ever felt before, but she was disturbed about something, and the name Ophelia kept ringing in her ear. She was at the point of wanting to scream!

Queen Faustina kept her big key ring in her hand. She rattled them as she looked around the area and saw how beautiful they were fixing everything in the place where she and Antoine wanted to get married. The rattle of her keys brought nothing to her mind. Especially the name Ophelia. She was beginning to hate the name. She wasn't going to name her little girl Ophelia that was for sure. She and Antoine hadn't thought about a name, but it was not going to be the name that was ringing in her ear!

Other Cajun Fairies were under the oak tree helping to fly tulle fabrics from one branch to the other. The braided rug road that was lined up straight in the middle of the land was super clean, and on each side of the road, it was trimmed with Miss Betty Lou's flowers of mixed colors. This was going to be the pathway for the Queen and Antoine to walk on, and then they would pass thought the archway of exotic flowers leading to the two statues under the big oak tree. Everything was set. They were just waiting for the fairy boat to return with the flowers for New Orleans.

Everyone was dressed in pink and white, even the sugar mill ladies. Marie La Vie who always wore white agreed she would wear pink. They always agreed with everything the Queen wanted, because she was such a fair and good queen. Anything they wanted they had. She was pleasant, but firm at times on some matters of etiquette and rules. She liked everyone to follow rules. But her rules were never too strict.

Madame Plume couldn't wait to wear pink. It was one of her favorite colors. She was always in white and she didn't want to out shine the Queen dressed in more white. How rude would that be, but Madame Poulette who always wore black, wasn't sure about being in pink. But, she looked above her glasses that were always on the tip of her nose and thought as she looked at herself in pink in the mirror, 'this was the Queen's BIG day' and she was going to do anything to please her. She was going to wear the pink dress. The stars would still surround her dress even if she was in pink.

Human time was getting closer to noon. They would eat, dance to the music of the Bebe Land Band, drink some wine that was made by Antoine, and merriment would fill the land under the big oak tree. Everything was ready. The chimes in the old oak tree were humming a sweet tune to the breeze.

Miss Betty Lou kept the dolls busy

with wedding decorations.

Chapter 2

The Gate into Lacey Laurel Lane

The fairy boat was docked in a cove at the levee by the river. It was hidden. No one knew about that place but the Cajun Fairies. They flew to Lacey Laurel Lane. They had no problem entering the lantern portal pole, and then they flew straight through the big, heavy, iron gate openings. There was no key to open this heavy gate. This was a place 'for dolls only'. The gate didn't even open. If a doll was too big to squeeze through the bars, they melted through. Humans never saw the big iron gate, because they didn't know about the portal lantern. The portal was the only way to get to the gate.

Instead of walking along Lacey Laurel Lane, they were flying over the pink brick road. This was only the second time they entered this place, and not being exactly sure where the shop "*Crystal Balls and All*" was, they first scoped out the area from above.

The place was filled with a maze of curved lanes. No corners at all like in the city. It was a continuous maze of pink brick curved roads with flowers everywhere. Spaced here and there along the curves in the brick road were circles with water fountains in them. There were shops with every accessory that a doll could want... a shop for purses, one for only gloves, and another for hats, fur coats, wigs, and shoes. Each shop had one specific item.

As they kept flying, they saw the curved lanes went further back. That back part of the lane was filled with magical shops. You could get magic wands, herbs, crystal balls, Ouija boards, scrying mirrors, mandrake plants... and that's only some of the things they saw in the shopping bags of many dolls. Just fascinating for them to see such sights.

The streets were filled with dolls from all over the world. It was indeed a marvelous land. There were porcelain dolls, cloth dolls, antique dolls, little spirit dolls, voodoo dolls, vinyl dolls, art dolls, even other fairy dolls. Every kind of doll you could imagine was dressed in their native clothes.

The further back they flew, dance halls and bars with lots of jazz music filled the air, until they reached a bayou. They didn't know there was a bayou in the back of Lacey Laurel Lane, but there it was, and only one house was set away from the land, on an island. The island wasn't part of the lanes, so they flew back to the shops.

They began their walk down the lane looking for the shop *Crystal Balls and All.*

At the door of each shop, they had what was called a belly yeller dressed in yellow and orange, calling out the items they had in the shop to sell. 'Hats in here. Get your hats in here'.

They laughed at the shop that said, 'Yodel tinker toy. Get your yodel tinker toy here'. Acadia almost went inside that shop just to see what it was, but they didn't want to be late bringing the Queen her pink silk flowers.

Lights made of thin white clouds floated over some of the streets, and each shop was painted in a different, vibrant color. But the most amazing thing they liked was a ballerina twirling at all times in front of each shop, softly saying... 'Welcome to Lacey Laurel Lane'. They repeated this over and over and it came out in a good tone throughout the place. Like the song of the land, the fairies thought. The place had a magnificent, magical atmosphere.

One thing they saw that was out of the ordinary were three small humans. They found this very strange, because this was a place where only dolls could enter, but they were disguised as cloth dolls. No one else noticed that they had *human* hands! The fairies saw their fingers. *Human* fingers hanging from long sleeves. The fairies kept walking and the small humans seemed to be following them. They were cautious about these three. The Queen told them the story about Lacey Laurel Lane, and no human knew about the portal lantern in the courtyard, and this was the only way to enter the big gate.

Finally, they found the shop, *Crystal Balls and All.*

Everything was free in this place unlike the city where they would need money. The doll land had no money. They lived a life free from all worries where magic ruled.

The Cajun Fairies got the pretty pink silk flowers that Queen Faustina wanted, placed a bunch in each a shopping bag, and flew out the shop. All the while they flew towards the iron gate to make their way back to the fairy boat at the levee, the three small humans watched them fly. It was strange that they watched only them. No other doll.

Two of the fairies swooped down near the three small humans while they were watching the other three fairies. They were all female with a lot of long hair set in braids, but one had a huge bouffant hairdo. It made her look like her head couldn't fit through any door. Two of them looked as though they could be twins with their rough look, but one had white hair and the other one had black hair. All of them had a rough look. Not a smile on any of their faces. But the one with the bouffant hairdo seemed to be the leader.

The fairies heard her speak for a few seconds and she was bossy. Even their voice sounded rough, deep for being female. Mean is the only word one fairy thought. They looked mean, dressed in their long dresses and carrying baskets filled with things from the shops. Whoever they were, they flew past them swiftly so they wouldn't be seen by them and joined the other three fairies.

On the way home from the shop, as they were pulling the fairy boat by the ropes that were attached because the inside of the boat was filled with pink silk flowers, the Cajun Fairies saw a strange pirogue ahead in an alley. This alley way was usually clear of all boat traffic. It was Swamp Alley, and this alley lead to other portals along the way, but not many knew about the portals.

One fairy flew over with a few egrets to get a closer look, and it was the same three strange looking small humans they saw at Lace Laurel Lane. They were paddling a wide pirogue. This fairy noticed that they all had moles on their faces. As their pirogue got closer to the fairy boat, they had to fly the boat up into a huge, empty eagles nest on an abandoned railcar track to avoid meeting up with them in the bayou. They kept very still as the pirogue was passing in the bayou under the track.

All of the fairies heard a voice saying, "You know, if Ophelia can get her hands on that Quizard that will be born today, we are the ones who will go and get her. She's always making us do her dirty work, but I can't wait to get that kid."

The voice had a bizarre sound like someone was speaking in a fan. One fairy whispered to the other, "She has a wavy voice, like someone is pinching her nose". The fairies had little munchkin's voices, but the small human voice was wavy and deep.

Queen Fairy Boat

"Yea, well she will need that Quizard by 3:33 pm, or the other one will go dim in 24 hours, and that's tomorrow at 3:33 pm. You can set your watch to that one, dearie! The legend says that Ophelia has one day to touch her skin."

"I'd like to see what Ophelia looks like if she didn't get a Quizard on time," snorted another small human. "Let's get back to the island as fast as we can. Ophelia will be angry with us if we're late."

"Their laugh sounds like a pig snort," whispered a fairy.

Their voices faded into the distance as the pirogue kept floating away from them under the track. They were snorting for as long as they could hear the voices. Snorting was their way of laughing and laughing. The little people never saw the fairy boat or the fairies. When they were out of sight, the fairy boat got right back into the bayou and completed what they had to do... bring the flowers to the doll land of Sha Bebe so the arch could be filled with the pretty pink silk flowers for the Queen. She loved those silk flowers, because the silk ones never die.

They made it home in plenty of time.

Wizard Antoine and Queen Faustina
under the arch of pink silk flowers.

The noon bell rang in the land and the Bebe Land Band began playing the wedding march. Surprisingly, to everyone standing there in their wedding clothes of pink and white, Queen Faustina and Wizard Antoine were under the beautiful archway in the clothes they normally wore. The band stopped.

"Faustina! Antoine!" Madame Plume was stunned. "You're not wearing the wedding clothes that my wand made for you! Where is your big, fluffy white dress? Antoine, no tuxedo? Why?"

"We don't know; do you know why Faustina?" They both looked at each other in amazement for at least a minute.

"No, I don't know where my wedding dress is," she looked at her pretty long dress she wore as Queen, "but I know I need to get married at noon." She didn't know why she said that either!

"Okay! The noon bell rang. We heard it ring," said Antoine. "The place is decorated so well. The food is ready, let's go on with the wedding." He bowed and sent them all a big smile.

Madame Plume gave him the squint eyes. All of her beautiful work was gone unseen by the rest in the land. This was not normal behavior for her Queen and her brother, the Wizard.

The Bebe Land Band started playing again, and the wedding march through the archway began. The ceremony went off beautifully. Not a mistake was made by anyone.

All of the 100 boys and girls were so well behaved, and the Queen and her Wizard said "I do" in front of the statues of Antoine's parents, Jacque and Evangeline. After they said "I do", they jumped a fancy-made broom covered with tulle wrapped around the broom, trimmed with more of those exotic pink silk flowers from that magical shop in New Orleans. It was indeed a joyous event, but even Marie La Vie was mystified at their behavior.

Sitting at the wedding table after the ceremony, Faustina and Antoine quickly got up and made a toast. "Cheers! Cheers to everyone in the doll land of Sha Bebe. Faustina and I raise our glasses to your happiness, and we thank you for this lovely wedding. We deeply appreciate everything you have done for us, and especially for accepting me into your land. Cheers!"

Everyone raised a glass and yelled, "CHEERS." The boys and girls raised small wine glasses filled with grape juice. As they were happily sipping to Antoine's gracious toast, he said, "Faustina and I want a girl child to be popped to life by Madame Plume's most powerful wand, at 3:33 pm on this 3rd day of the 12th month in human time. TODAY... and ... CHEERS!" He smiled with a big grin as he raised his glass again.

Madame Plume spit her drink out, and everyone else choked!

"WHAT? Both of you want a girl child, today?"

"Not now, Plume. At 3:33 pm today. CHEERS!" Antoine said again, smiling. Everyone was indeed happy, but shocked.

"Are you drunk, Antoine?" Madame Plume was flustered. Queen Faustina had a big grin on her face too. "Faustina, do you want a girl child at 3:33 TODAY, like in three hours from now?"

"Yes, I do. I don't know why, but yes, what a splendid idea. CHEERS!"

"WELL, okay! If that's what you both want," said Madame Plume shrugging her shoulders and slapping the feathers on her dress in frustration, "but we sure won't be partying and dancing until the early morning hours." She was astounded at this news.

Madame Poulette and Marie La Vie were just standing there, speechless, and Madame Plume swiftly turned around shaking her feathered dress almost to pieces. She was going to eat cake! She mumbled to herself. "No wedding clothes on their wedding day. They said I do, CHEERS, and then, 'we want a girl child.' It makes no sense to me. What's the hurry?"

Something wasn't right, but she wanted to eat cake! In only three hours, she had to POP a girl child to life for the Queen and her brother. Taking a bite of the delicious cake made by the sugar mill ladies, Plume raised her glass of wine to Madame Poulette and Marie La Vie and said, "CHEERS!"

Both of them walked over to join Madame Plume, just shaking their head. They chatted for a little while about this surprise announcement, at their wedding of all places, and then everyone ate cake and danced.

Chapter 3

The Birth of a Quizard

Antoine set a big clock for 3:00 pm. He made this huge clock with the magic in his hands and it was hung on the big oak tree. All of Queen Faustina's door knob chimes blew gently in the wind, and they made a joyous melody for their vows.

When the huge clock hit 3:00 pm everything shifted into forward gear.

The Queen and the Wizard announced that everyone at the wedding had to rush on over the Madame Plume's pink plantation home for the birth of a little girl at 3:33. The time had to be exact, and he had a pocket watch also on his side.

Everything was happening so quickly.

Madame Plume, Marie La Vie, and Madame Poulette watched in amazement as Miss Betty Lou gathered the 100 boys and girls to run over to Plume's house at the other end of the braided rug road. The 16 sugar mill ladies helped her.

"Why do we hurry?" Marie La Vie asked in her deep Cajun accent. "Never before do I feel so rushed!"

Madame Plume took another bite of wedding cake. "I don't know, but they said at 3:33 pm and they are rushing to my home at 3:00 pm. Makes no sense at all to me. This is not what I expected today." She rushed on over to her own home with the rest of them. Her feathers were flying in every direction as she ran to catch up with the rest.

"Wait for me, Faustina! I need to be there for the birth you know." Now, she was running. "HEY, wait for me!"

When Plume got to her front door, everyone in the land was at the "birthing table" where she POPPED all of the dolls to life. Miss Betty Lou told the 100 boys and girls outside and the Queen and the Wizard would show them the baby girl when it was time. Some sat on the swing and on the big front porch, some played in the trees, and others just sat on the grounds.

"Okay, POP our little girl to life Plume, it's almost 3:33 pm," Wizard Antoine said with an excitement in his voice like Plume had never heard before. Queen Faustina was all smiles too, the biggest grin she had ever seen on her face. Ever!

"Okay," Plume said, trying to calm herself down. "I'm usually in this room alone with my wand at the "birthing table", but beings this is a very special occasion, welcome to all of you who are here to witness the birth of the newest little Princess in the land... and also my niece." Madame Plume took a bow. "Now, if everyone could just push back a little and give me and my fabrics some room, I'll get started with my magic wand."

The way that Madame Plume POPPED the dolls to life had never changed since the beginning of time. She twirled her magic wand over her head. When she did this, all of her fabrics that filled the birthing room on every wall in the huge room, from the top of the ceiling to the bottom shelf on the floor would spin swiftly around the huge room overhead in a circular motion. The magic wand made the fabrics spin around the room. Madame Plume was the best doll artist around. She was well known in every doll land for her raggedy chic looking dolls.

The residents watched in amazement. So many fabrics were twirling overhead, that they could not see the birthing table at all. But Madame Plume knew what she was doing.

This went on for a few minutes, and finally the mass of twirling fabrics began to thin out, slowing down, and each piece went back to the shelf they were in when the twirling began.

On the birthing table, at 3:33 pm ... there she was. The first Princess of the Land of Sha Bebe, officially made by Madame Plume. The little girl stood up on the table.

Madame Plume screamed. Queen Faustina fell to her knees. Antoine caught his Queen. Marie La Vie put her hands on her cheeks and said 'Oh Mon Gris-Gris'! Miss Betty Lou and Madame Poulette just stood there with their mouths wide open. The 16 sugar mill ladies backed up and stood perfectly still.

"What happened?" Madame Plume was stunned!

"I'll go and zap a very special magic flying quilt for our new little Princess," was all that Madame Poulette could say as she left the room quickly to make her a special white blanket, fit for a Princess with fringes on all four sides.

The 16 sugar mill ladies said they were going to fix the wedding table outside with more food and drinks as they left the room.

Miss Betty Lou went into the yard and gathered the 100 boys and girls to go back to the wedding table to enjoy more cake and music. Some of them wanted to see the new Princess, but Miss Betty Lou told them that when the Queen and the Wizard were going to be ready, they would make their announcement. It would be a very special announcement. She told them, "Let's wait and see. We'll all be surprised at the same time."

Meanwhile, Madame Poulette came running back into the birthing room with an exquisite white blanket to give to the new Princess. She made it especially for her. She was saving this white piece of fabric to make herself a shawl, but she wanted the Princess to have it.

The only residents in the room now were the Queen and the Wizard, sitting near the birthing table, Madame Plume, Madame Poulette, Marie La Vie and two Cajun fairies, Acadia and Olivia. No one said a word. The silence was deafening.

Madame Poulette broke that silence and said, "Awe Sha, come with me little Princess, you need to meet your mama and your daddy. You're beautiful."

She put the little girl in the pretty white blanket that she had just made, and then she handed her to the Queen and the Wizard. Queen Faustina and Wizard Antoine looked at their little girl and then they both looked at Plume.

"Why is she blue? Is she okay? She is beautiful, but I have never seen a blue doll before in any land."

Marie La Vie knew why and she answered. "She's what you call a Quizard. She comes only to a real Queen and a true Wizard. Very rare. Yes! Very rare. Such a wonderful event for me to see. I never saw a Quizard before now." Marie La Vie was elated and continued to stand with her arms crossed as she observed this beautiful event.

"There is a magic key somewhere in this land, because a Quizard is born."

The Princess was born at 3:33 pm

Madame Plume shrugged her shoulders, not knowing what to say, and she didn't hear what Marie La Vie announced. No one heard Marie La Vie. They kept looking at the blue doll.

Plume began to cry. "I don't know what happened! Maybe it

was all of the rushing. Maybe the fabrics felt rushed. The fabrics are used to a quiet room with no one here but me. Maybe my wand is failing me … Oh … I'm so sorry. She is so beautiful! Look at her regal clothes!" Plume was wiping her tears, and crying uncontrollably.

The Wizard got up from his chair and hugged his sister. She still had her wand in her hand while she was crying, and she hugged Antoine back.

"She is beautiful Antoine! LOOK, she has your pointed eyes. Oh my goodness! Her eyes are white, but she's beautiful. My wand has never made a doll that looked this different, and my wand make many, many dolls, as you know. You do know that, right?"

"Yes, I know."

Madame Plume was beginning to feel a little better now that Antoine gave his approval. She looked at the Queen. "Faustina, how do you feel? Are you okay? She's a special doll, you must admit that."

"Oh, I love her deeply. She's what the wand wanted us to have. I wouldn't want another doll but this one. It was just that initial shock of seeing a blue doll, and I my knees got weak for a second or two, but I adore her."

The little girl was hugging Faustina, and then she went to her daddy and gave him a hug. They were delighted about her caring ways.

"Can Aunt Plume get a hug? I made you special." Madame Plume had her arms outstretched ready for her hug. At that moment, her wand went haywire. The wand was controlling her, not the other way around.

"What's happening? I can't let go of my wand!" She was out of control. Her hand with the wand was going up and down, left and right. All of her fabrics began flying overheard, and twirling in a circle faster than before.

The Wizard picked up his little girl and handed her to the Queen while he held on tightly to Faustina. Madame Poulette and Marie La Vie again watched in amazement. Acadia and Olivia flew low and stayed next to the front door. It was like a tornado of fabrics in the birthing room. As abruptly as the fabrics began flying overhead, it ended. And there on the table was another girl Princess, as normal as all of the 100 boys and girls who were playing in the yard.

Complete silence filled the room again. Marie La Vie kept still and watched with her two hands clasped inside each other. The mole that she was born with between her eyes felt nothing evil going on. Marie La Vie would have felt evil from what she called her third eye, and she had a pleasant feeling inside of her while she smiled.

"Okay! I didn't do this!" Plume spoke up. Her wand had never in all the time she had made dolls, took it upon itself to make a doll without her leading the fabrics to do so. Ever! But there she was … another girl Princess, and only 3 minutes after the first one.

"Is this one our little girl too?" asked the Queen, holding the first one close to her.

"I have no idea. Your guess is as good as mine. This has never happened before!" Madame Plume put her wand down on the chair before another doll would POP to life.

The second Princess got down from the table on her own, and ran to the first Princess and gave her a hug saying, "Maggie, you're here!"

"Molly! Yes, I made it to the doll land with the help of Madame Plume's magic wand. I was waiting for you."

They embraced on the Queen's lap for what seemed to be an entire minute.

Again, the silence was broken by Madame Poulette. "TWINS. I tell you, it is twin Princesses. Awe Sha, and they are both beautiful. Welcome Princess Maggie and Princess Molly."

"How can they be twins Poulette, they don't even look alike?" Plume was so confused.

"They are twins because they know each other. What else could this be?" said Madame Poulette. "Maggie already knows Molly."

Immediately, Maggie and Molly began playing in the room

The Queen and the Wizard got caught up in the moment of their daughters playing together as if they knew each other before. They were running around the birthing table, examining each other's clothing, looking at each other's faces, not ever saying one word about how one was blue and the other was white.

Maggie was dressed in a long black velvet dress trimmed with silver sequins. Her hair was salt and pepper, not rag hair, and she had the shiny, glittery, triangle eyes of her dad. Molly was dressed the same as the Queen, her dress filled with lace, flowers and ribbons in her hair, and she had blue eyes like the Queen.

When Queen Faustina and Wizard Antoine saw that the two girls got along well and seemed to be a part of each other, like they had known each other before, they decided to go outdoors and announce the twin birth to the rest of the residents and the boys and girls. They were waiting to see the new Princess, but no one was expecting to see two Princesses.

"Marie, you do the honors," said Queen Faustina.

Marie La Vie stood at the front door and made the birth

announcement. With her two hands clasped together she said, "The Queen and the Wizard have twin girls! One is a Quizard, born to only a real Queen and a true Wizard. Her skin is blue. She is very rare. The second twin girl is not a Quizard. More needs to be done for a Quizard to get her magic. We have 24 hours to do this. But first let me introduce the new Princesses to the Doll Land of Sha Bebe."

Marie La Vie then, opened the door in grand style, bowing. The two Princesses stepped outside looking at the crowd in the land. Antoine and Faustina came out on the porch to tell the crowd how happy they were about their beautiful girls, Princess Maggie, a Quizard who was born first, and her twin sister Princess Molly who was born three minutes after. Madame Plume and Madame Poulette also took a bow while listening to Antoine and Faustina speak about their beautiful girls.

After the announcement, the twin girls went under the oak tree and played. Not one of the other boys and girls said anything about Maggie's blue skin which made her different from all of the tan, white, black, and brown dolls. They played together, ate cake, and went on as though nothing new had happened except two more dolls were born in the land of Sha Bebe by the magic of Madame Plume's wand.

Marie La Vie pulled Antoine and Faustina aside. "The Quizard has 24 hours to find her magic. I think we stay and keep going with the festivities of your wedding for a few hours, and then we need to end the ceremony. There is a secret I need to tell you."

"Is everything okay with our little Princesses?" Faustina looked worried.

"Oh yes," smiled Marie La Vie. "Everything could not be better than this. We all spend another few hours outdoors and when the girls go to bed, we talk."

The Queen and the Wizard had great trust in the wisdom of

Marie La Vie, so they did as she suggested. They stayed outdoors for two more hours, and then the celebration ended.

Everyone went back to their respected homes. The sugar mill ladies cleaned up everything with the help of the magic wand of Madame Poulette. The dance of the flying plates went in reverse from the way they did at the dinner table in the dining room. The wand cleaned all of the dishes on the table, then with the wisp of her wand all of the plates danced back into the kitchen house. Napkins and linens were neatly stored away. The tulle and flower arrangements were picked up and neatly placed near the statues of Jacque and Evangeline. The doll land was back in order. Same as it was before the festivities. Everyone was asleep, but there were two additions who would live in the land. Princess Maggie, and Princess Molly.

Chapter 4

The Haunted House of Dr. Ophelia Amedee

The name Ophelia that was buzzing inside of Queen Faustina's mind before the wedding had gone away with the birth of her twin girls. Her joy at seeing her girls playing under the big oak tree and getting along with the other boys and girls had over taken her worry of the name. But Ophelia was very real, and she was very much aware of the birth of a Quizard. She sent her three dwarf minions to spray a formula in the air through a hole they made in the invisible dome around the land of Sha Bebe. This formula is what caused all of the rush and confusion.

The Queen was right about her strange feelings. Dr. Ophelia Amedee needed a Quizard to stay alive. The Quizard she had now was fading away. Only Marie La Vie knew about the legend of the Quizard and the magical doorknob key chime.

Ophelia was an eccentric witch doctor. She never liked dolls. She thought they were pesky little toys that gave her a creepy feeling. A nuisance. She didn't know the dolls of the land of Sha Bebe were alive like her Quizard. All of them. Not just one doll.

Ophelia was not a doll. She was human. As an only child born into a well-to-do family in New Orleans, they made their money from owning most of the sugar cane fields in the country land outside of the city, along with owning the sugar mills. She was raised in one of the richest mansions on prestigious St. Charles Avenue and her parents spoiled her rotten. Anything she wanted they bought her. She was sassy to her parents and also to the servants. The house was always full of servants. The pristine lawn was always filled with gardeners. She made all of them serve her, hand and foot.

Her parents attended and hosted many fabulous balls in their luxurious home, but none of this impressed Ophelia. She didn't like the affluent friends of her family. She had the best clothes made especially for her by the finest seamstresses, but she didn't feel beautiful in any gown that was ever made for her. The servants said she was born under a bad moon and she was destined to be a spoiled brat with no kindness inside of her at all.

When she was a toddler she had a cute moon pie face, but as she grew older, she acquired a homely look. She was not a beauty, but she wanted to be beautiful. She was smart but there was a loopy side to her that no one could figure out. Her parents kept telling her she was their beauty queen, but she knew they were doing this just to please her.

Not one boy in all of her years at school ever told her she was pretty, much less beautiful. All they did was laugh at her. It never occurred to her that people didn't like her ill-mannered nature, and that she was intolerable to be around. At an early age she thought the family money could buy her anything she wanted. In Ophelia's controlling mind, everything was always done *her way* or it was not done at all. She always had the last word.

When she was old enough she enrolled in Tulane University to learn about medicines and chemistry. Her narcissistic mind thought that if she could major in chemistry, she could invent some kind of formula to make herself beautiful. *'Oh my, I will be more popular!'* she thought. She knew there was no beauty cream or makeup artist that could give her what she wanted. She had tried them all. Even though she was good for business in many shops in the city, most of the salons said they were always booked, just so they didn't have to deal with her drama sessions in the "beauty chair", as she called it, while insulting them with each hair style they fixed for her.

No one liked her. When she walked down the streets in New Orleans, most shop owners would cringe at the sight of her coming in for clothes. She was insulting, intolerable, and mean. Just down right mean!

Ophelia managed to get a degree in chemistry by cheating. She loved mixing herbs for different potions, so she opened an alternative medicine shop in the city. She would be a doctor of herbal medicines. It didn't work out well at all. She accidentally poisoned one of her patients, and she nearly died. That costs her parents a big chunk of money, and she closed her office. Everyone in the city called here a quack.

She told her parents, who were worn out trying to please her that she wanted to open a small beauty shop. They indulged her again and again. She found the shop she wanted, right next door to a Voodoo shop on Decatur Street in New Orleans. She liked this shop more than any other shop in the city. It was there that she began drinking. Rum and coke was her drink. She was hooked on it the minute she took her first sip. Later, she learned how to make the rum on her own, as well as many other potions that she bought from that shop.

The Voodoo Queen who managed the Voodoo shop called her a drunken quack doctor with no potential at all. "You don't take anything in your life seriously, Ophelia. One day you will be drowning in your own spit, and no one will be able to help you. You will be all alone."

She didn't like Ophelia, so she performed a *stay away spell* on her. She had enough of her! She mixed a dark blue dye in some grounded bricks that she picked up at an old tomb outside the cemetery. The Voodoo Queen would never steal, even from the dead. When she took the bricks, she left coins. She added a few strands of Ophelia's hair that she has snipped off when she was in one of her drunken stupors, and sprinkled the blue brick mixture at Ophelia's shop door.

After she laid the *stay away spell* at Ophelia's door, she laid her *drawing dust* in front of her own door. She mixed some red brick dust with cinnamon powder, brown sugar, and water. She scrubbed her floor at the doorway inside of her shop for a quick and continuous cash flow.

After Ophelia opened her beauty shop, her parents asked her to go on a trip with them to Egypt. "Come with us dear. It will be such fun."

She declined. In a big way they were relieved that she didn't want to go, because they knew she wasn't going to enjoy the trip, and they needed a break away from her.

She was growing angrier with each day that passed by. No one came to her beauty shop. No one wanted to buy her products. People were flocking to the Voodoo Queen, but none came to her shop. Ophelia took a step towards the Voodoo shop to ask the lady why no one was coming to see *her*, and she stayed right where she was standing on the street. The Voodoo lady's spell worked.

Not one job that Ophelia tried ever worked out well for her. She felt this way about her whole life ever since she was a child. The servants at her parents' home were right when they said she was born under a bad moon, and she was destined to be a spoiled brat with no kindness inside of her at all. But to Ophelia, it was always someone else's fault for the way her life turned out.

Three weeks later, a messenger was sent to the family home to let Ophelia know that her parents were killed in an airplane crash on the way home from Egypt. She was speechless. The servants were speechless. No more parents? Who would she argue with now? She made all the necessary funeral arrangements with no emotions at all, went to the reading of the will, and this is when she found out she was the sole heir to everything her parents had. She had no family members. None at all. No aunts. No uncles. Not even a cousin. She was sure that here parents would have left the servants something, but no, so she let them go. No paychecks for them. She just yelled at them to leave the house.

In her dismal state of mind, she decided to sell everything that her parents left her and move away from the city. When her affairs were in order, she moved further south into the marshlands, until she found an island with an old house on it. It seemed to be in good shape, so she bought the entire island. She lived alone on that deserted island. No one to bother her. No one to make fun of her. Oh my, no more servants to get mad at? She didn't think about that!

When she was moving all of her belongings into the old house on the island by boat, she met up with three dwarf sisters at the dock who were looking for a job cleaning houses. She hired them on the spot, and took them into her home immediately. She couldn't bear the thought of having no one to yell at, but the sisters didn't know that she was so mean and controlling.

Well, there was Cromwell for her to yell at. He was a mummy who roamed around Ophelia since she was a child. He came out of a sarcophagus that her parents had for many years from another country, and Ophelia named him Cromwell. They never got along well and Ophelia screamed back at him when he screamed at her. Both were ornery old beings, but the three sisters would work out just fine as servants.

Cornwell enjoyed the company he kept with the three dwarf sisters more than he did with Ophelia. She didn't let them leave the island when they first moved in. Ophelia was too afraid they would never come back to live with her.

But as time went by, the three sisters, named Clotilda, Matilda, and Emelda Crumbpacker became very used to the old house on the island, and Ophelia's money, so they stayed. They did all of the work around the place as well as serving Ophelia hand and foot. Ophelia liked Emelda the best. It was Emelda who she told all of her secrets to. Mostly about her miserable life. Emelda was her confidante. As the years went by, she let the sister go shopping for her. Ophelia knew they had no other place to go and make the money she paid them.

The old house was also haunted by the spirit of a small child. Many people didn't want to go around that old house because of the haunted legend of a little girl who lived there and died in the well. The parents of the child thought she was kidnapped when no clues were found. But the well was very deep, and she died at the bottom of it. The police looked in the well, but never saw her little body. In their grief for their little girl, they moved away, leaving the once beautiful house, haunted with the ghost of their little girl. No one ever saw her, except Cromwell.

Boats that navigated around the island said they could hear a voice screaming the word --- *daddy*. Ophelia heard the little girl's voice also, but wasn't bothered by it. Nothing bothered Ophelia but the way she looked. She still wanted to be beautiful.

Many years went by. She grew older and homelier. One day she screamed, "No more mirrors in the house. Emelda, take them all out!" Emelda and her sisters took all of them down and put them in the attic. Ophelia saw warts coming out on her face. Ophelia's life was filled with mourning, anger, and misery all of which she brought on herself. She never caught on to the fact that beauty began inside of a person not outside.

As she aged, she looked like a humpback old lady. She was always dressed in loose fitting clothes which added to her age. Her hair was pulled back into a mishmash style of what was supposed to be a bun. She had given up on beauty. For the past year, all she was doing was arguing with Cromwell, and telling the ghost girl in the well to shut up! She had brainwashed the three dwarf sisters with her stash of money into thinking they were her slaves. They stayed for the money, but Ophelia had no empathy for them at all and was filled with self-hate.

One weekend, on a whim, she decided she wanted to see Hawaii, so she booked a flight. When she landed in Hawaii, it was there that she saw her first Quizard. She was on display at the airport. The blue doll was walking, dancing, and talking to all of the people who passed by, and the people would leave the old man some money in a jar.

Ophelia was especially amazed that this cloth doll could walk and talk, but when she bent down take a closer look at the doll, the doll touched Ophelia's arm. Immediately she felt a tingle on her skin, a prickly feeling. She noticed it on her arms first. Then the tingly feeling went to every part of her body. When that feeling got to her head, she felt dizzy. Thinking the doll had some sort of disease, she was going to approach the old man to give him a piece of her mind about the blue doll touching her, and to keep her on a leash. As she leaned in towards the old man to tell him, she felt taller. She quickly straightened up. Suddenly she felt her body transform. The hump on her back was gone.

She ran to a shop nearby and when she looked into a mirror, her face and her hair were different! Everything on her was changing right before her eyes. She watched the transformation in the shop mirror. A mirror! She hadn't looked at herself in a mirror for decades.

She transformed from a frumpy old lady, into a sultry, jet black haired woman, with the figure of a pin up girl. She watched in the mirror as her old clothes melted into a long, black, satin gown. Ophelia looked beautiful! She was beyond amazed. Flabbergasted is what she was. Flabbergasted!

Going back to the old man, she asked him how much for the blue doll. She would pay him any amount of money he wanted.

He told her she was not for sale. She was called a Quizard, *very rare*, born of a Queen and a Wizard. He told Ophelia that he found her crying in the woods all alone. She had no home, so he kept her as his own. He was firm in his answer to Ophelia, and she got mad.

After arguing with the old man who still insisted the blue doll was not for sale, Ophelia stole her and brought her back home on the plane. On the plane ride home she found out from the doll that she had magic in her blue skin, but the magic only lasted for 50 years, and she only had 10 years left. All Ophelia heard her say was she had 10 years left to feel her skin and enjoy her beauty.

She admitted to Ophelia there was more to the magic she possessed but she couldn't remember everything the old man told her. Ophelia paid her no mind. She sat in her seat and looked at herself in a compact mirror she bought at the airport. She was still flabbergasted at how she looked.

The plane landed in New Orleans, and she immediately went to a photographer. The best studio she knew in the city. She had photos of herself taken to hang all over the house. Large photos in huge frames. She and the blue doll spent the night in a posh New Orleans hotel until the photos were ready the next day. She locked the blue doll in the hotel room and left to sashay the streets of New Orleans.

People admired her sultry walk. Men whistled at her, asked her if she wanted a drink in a local night club, told her she was beautiful. Everything she always wanted to hear, she heard in one night. For one blissful night, she felt like she was alive. No yelling.

No hatred. No meanness. She soaked up every word of praise that she heard people say about her. Ophelia finally felt adored. It was her dream come true.

When she went back to the hotel room, it didn't take much to bring out the old Ophelia when a lady told her that her shoes were gross. She was fuming in that fancy hotel lobby. She simply told the uppity lady that she had no taste in fashion and went up to her room. The blue doll was asleep, so Ophelia didn't disturb her and she went to bed also, still mad at the shoe incident. That blissful night was to be her only moment of happiness.

When she got home with the blue doll, the three dwarf sisters didn't know who was coming to the house. They sent Cromwell outside to check out the "new lady". When the new lady yelled at Cromwell to move out of her way, he knew it was Ophelia. He jetted back into the house and screamed, "It's her!"

The second she stepped inside of the house she yelled at Emelda to get her a drink. "Look at me Emelda, I'm beautiful!"

Emelda was in shock and got her a rum and coke. Matilda and Clotilda were looking from the door in the next room. The three of them were in totally disbelief at the transformation of Ophelia. The sound of her voice was the same, and her attitude was no different at all, but to see her standing there, looking beautiful in that long black dress, compared to the way she looked when she left to go to Hawaii, it was like night and day. It took them a week to get used to accepting this "new lady" in the old house. Cromwell and the ghost girl ran in the yard and stayed near the well.

She treated the blue doll very well for a while because she made her look beautiful. This doll gave her what she has always wanted. Beauty! She told Emelda, Clotilda and Matilda to give her anything she wanted. She was special. Emelda was told to immediately hang all of her mirrors back on the walls. All three dwarfs were hurrying to fulfill Ophelia's every wish. Mirrors filled the house again.

Ophelia realized right then and there, that she could go to the city and walk the streets of New Orleans without people laughing at her, but ten years would go by quickly, and her beauty would fade. She knew she would need to go on another trip to find another Quizard at some point in time, but as of now, she was going to enjoy her new life. She had ten years. That's all she wanted to know. Everything was always about her!

Ten years passed by, and in those years, Ophelia assembled a radar room in the old haunted house She filled the room with devices for detecting Queens and Wizards from every part of the world. She had the best equipment money could buy. The room lit up like a festive tree during the holidays. There were low sounds of beeps and dings filling the room day and night. Emelda was in charge of the radar room. When the radar spotted a location where there was a Queen and a Wizard, a low alarm would go off. There were many Queens and Wizards scattered around the planet on the big screen, but none were married.

Every morning Ophelia woke up and checked to see if there were any marriages to beget a Quizard, and each morning there were only faint sounds foretelling that a Quizard was coming soon, but when? Where? She didn't know.

She began thinking that the old man in Hawaii lied to her, or he told her a legend that wasn't true. She asked the Quizard she owned again what the old man told her, and her story was always the same. She insisted he said she came from a real Queen and a true Wizard.

There was a deep secret to the magic of the Quizard that Ophelia didn't know, because the Quizard didn't know the deep secret, either. Her Quizard only knew that she was born at 3:33 on the 12th month, because she was separated from her parents at some point. She didn't know how she ended up in the woods, but she was glad the old man found her. She was happy with him, but now she was stuck in her dreary world with Ophelia. No one knew the secret of the Quizard and the magic inside the blue doll except Marie La Vie.

Ophelia needed a Quizard to keep her alive, because after so many wonderful years of enjoying her beauty from the magic of her Quizard, if she couldn't stay young, she didn't want to live. She didn't know if her heart would have been defective after ten years and just stop beating. Her kidneys, her liver!

There would be no more partying and travels all over the world. Every day she could feel the magic in her Quizard fading away. The tingle she felt all over her body when she first took her in Hawaii was not the same. She never talked to her Quizard anymore. She didn't even know her name! She kept here in one room in the old house and her activities were very limited. Ten years had gone by and her Quizard played with Cromwell and the ghost girl only. She never left the island.

A thought occurred to her. What would she do with the old Quizard when a new Quizard would arrive? She was of no use to her anymore, and she was certain that a new Quizard would arrive soon, because the alarms in the radar room got louder as each day went by, but she didn't know where she would need to travel to get her new Quizard.

She sat down a while to think about this. She couldn't throw her away after all her years of service. She gave her beauty. As she kept thinking and drinking, a solution came to her mind. She would have Emelda drop her off at Lacey Laurel Lane. She would blend in with the other dolls there. Someone would take her in, for sure. That was the only nice thought that Ophelia ever had. The old Quizard would live at Lacey Laurel Lane.

She made the old Quizard two dolls from moss that she picked out of the trees. These would be her playmates if no one wanted a blue faced doll. This was the only act of kindness they ever saw from Ophelia. Kindness was never inside of her.

Emelda did as Ophelia told her.

One night when it was getting dark, Emelda left with a lantern in her hand, while Clotilda and Matilda paddled the pirogue to the back of the bayou to Lacey Laurel Lane. When they got the pirogue to land, they said goodbye to the old Quizard. They watched her walk down the pink brick road, holding her two moss dolls while everyone was asleep. When they couldn't see her anymore, they went back home. No remorse at all.

Ophelia made the old Quizard two moss dolls to play
with just in case no one wanted a blue faced doll.
She was waiting for her new Quizard with great anticipation.

Two days later, all of her sophisticated radar equipment lights went off loudly on her board in the radar room. An event showed up on the screen. There was going to be a wedding for a Queen and a Wizard. Ophelia was elated!

"Where is this place?"

Emelda began pulling levels and clicking knobs, and saw on

the big screen that it was not far from the island. "Here it is! Just a boat ride away."

"Why didn't I know about this land of dolls?"

"I don't know," said Emelda in her squeaky little child-like voice as she kept clicking knobs. "It seems they have some sort of shield around the place."

Ophelia swung her long dress around. "Well, we'll see about that! The three of you will break that shield. I'll mix up a potion that will burn a hole in that shield. I learned a lot being next to that Voodoo shop in New Orleans. The three of you will get in that land through that hole at night and take the Quizard when she is born. It will be a girl!"

Ophelia was dancing around the room in a way that the dwarf sisters had never seen her dance before. Being a little shocked that she was happy for a change, Emelda went to check the bottles of rum, and there was one empty. She was drunk and happy. The three dwarfs sat down and watched, because they knew they would never see that again.

Now that she knew where a Queen and a Wizard were getting married, Ophelia had enough time to plan how she was going to take her new Quizard. The night before the wedding she would put a spell on the Queen and the Wizard to make them want a girl child quickly… right after the wedding vows. The spell would cause much confusion inside of the Queen and the Wizard's mind. The three dwarf sisters would be watching the whole thing through a hole in the invisible shield with a potion that Ophelia had made called a *sleeping snuff*. When it would be dark, after everyone was asleep, the three of them would enter the land. They would take the Quizard after she smelled the *sleeping snuff*. It was the best plan Ophelia had ever put together.

She sent her three dwarf minions to stalk the land of Sha Bebe weeks ahead of the wedding. No one could enter the land. Since the beginning of time there was an invisible dome surrounding the entire sugar cane field acreage that was occupied by the Sha Bebe. Over the years, only twice had someone penetrated the invisible dome wall. Bagasse Man got in twice, and the wicked Cajun Fairy, Robes Pierre, broke through. Other than that, the land was very secure with the protection of the invisible dome wall surrounding it. The Ugly Babies came into the land through a portal. That was a horrible time for the doll land, but the wall was not broken. Now that Ophelia was aware of the invisible wall, she would be the third one to penetrate it.

Ophelia told Emelda, "This is so convenient. In a few days, I'll have a baby Quizard, and it will be almost right next door to me. I bought all of this fancy equipment for nothing. Go figure. Is everything ready for the wedding day?"

"Yes, it is. The hole in the invisible dome is open large enough for us to get inside the land."

Ophelia cackled. "And my sleeping snuff is all bottled up. All you and your sisters need to do once you get inside the doll land is put some of the tonic I made near the nose of the new Princess, and MY new Quizard will be out like a light."

"The boat is ready, and we're ready. Can't wait to see a new blue doll here, myself." Emelda had become almost as wicked as Ophelia. Almost.

Ophelia took another drink. "I don't have to travel far to get this one." She sat in her favorite chair, put her feet up against the wall, and kept drinking. All she wanted to do now was look at one of the big photo she had made of herself and relish the moment. No more worries about getting older. She would have her Quizard in time.

The Voodoo Queen in New Orleans was right. She was a narcissistic, drunk, quack doctor, with no potential. The house was full of empty bottles. When she was woozy enough from drinking, she looked at her big photo and said to herself, "Oh, Ophelia, you are Beautimus. Simply *BEAUTIMUS*!" She got out of her chair, spun around the room with Emelda, and began singing.

I'm so Beautimus.

Oh so Beautimus.

No one can take away my looks.

Let them try. Let them try.

Oh, let them try. La la la….

I will surely make them cry…... La la la la la

Clotilda and Matilda were in the next room and heard everything. "I told you she was going to make us go and get that new Quizard. I told you! I know her like the back of my hand."

Ophelia adored the photo she took for Mardi Gras.

It was her prize photo, and she enjoyed having no family ties.

She was a loner who only needed someone to demonize.

BUT -- She was about to learn about the Sha Bebe.

From a doll land she knew nothing about.

She still hated dolls, but these dolls were not just any dolls.

They were a family of dolls.

And as a family, they always stuck together, no matter what.

Unlike most human families.

Chapter 5

The Secret of the Magical Doorknob Chime

The twins were asleep, and it was time for Marie La Vie to tell the secret of the magic key to the new parents of a Quizard. There was now only 20 hours left for the Princess Maggie to gain her magical powers. Queen Faustina and Wizard Antoine went into the living room after they tucked in Maggie and Molly for the night. Marie sat with them in the living room and began to tell them what she knew. Everyone in the land was used to her heavy Cajun accent.

"What I am going to tell you is a legend that is old. I heard many legends of all kind, and I see many strange things happen in my life, but I never saw a Quizard before now. I am honored to be here with you two for this rare event."

"Marie, why are you so formal about this birth just because Princess Maggie is blue?" asked Faustina. "I want her to be raised the same way as Princess Molly. Not different."

"Oh, but they will never be the same. Oh no. They are different. They know they are different, and they know they are twins by chance. I don't know what the chance is why one is blue and the other one is white, but there is a deep meaning behind this that none of us know yet. I deeply believe the both of them know why Molly is here. They should both be born blue."

Marie La Vie took a deep breath and put her head down, "Molly is here for a certain reason."

"We're all here for a reason," said Antoine. "I understand your joy. We're overjoyed at the births, but both girls will be raised the same, as Faustina said."

"And they should, but I need to tell you the legend of the Quizard."

Antoine and Faustina sat on the couch to listen. Marie La Vie sat on the high back settee.

"Listen to me! Maggie is a Quizard, and only a Quizard has the blue skin. She has magic powers. I don't know what powers she got now. She will know this as she grows up, but for her to get her power, there is a magic doorknob key in the land, or there would be no Quizard born here. The key that hangs from the doorknob needs to be turned in the keyhole 24 hours after a Quizard is born or she loses the magic that she has coming to her. We need to find the magic key."

"I have at least a dozen or more doorknob key chimes in my oak tree in the front yard, Marie!" Queen Faustina was very excited about this news. "Let's go and look!"

"Wait, Faustina. I have not finished telling you the secret to the *Turning of the Key* ritual. It's called... The Blue Chant."

"Oh, a ritual?" She loved rituals.

"Yes. The Quizard is born with the blue skin because they

have a blue heart. When the key is turned in the doorknob keyhole, it lights the blue light inside the heart, and when the key is popped out after saying The Blue Chant, she is filled with the magic she deserves." Marie stood up and began walking with her hands clasped together.

"Only a Queen and a Wizard can have a Quizard. Legend says that her blue skin and her magic powers stay with her for 50 years, and then the three of you need to be together again after 50 years to turn the key and say The Blue Chant again. This is why a Quizard is so rare."

Marie continued. "Many times the magic key is separated from the doorknob and some don't know how to protect the doorknob and the key. Sometime the Quizard leaves the Queen and the Wizard and they need to all be there; the three together for the Blue Chant. Sometime they lose the writings of the Blue Chant. Some don't know the legend at all and think they have a bad baby! Too sad. So many things can go wrong and change in 50 years. I hear the story two times in my life, but this is the first time, for me, that I see a Quizard be born. Amazing for me to see."

"Will she have magical powers like me?" Antoine's face was aglow.

"I don't know. She knows her magic power. Each Quizard has

different powers."

The Queen said, "I have no magic. But my intuition is strong. For the love of Sha Bebe, she is rare!"

The legend of a Quizard was beginning to sink in. Queen Faustina took a deep breath. "How about Molly?"

"No, Molly is the normal Sha Bebe. Only Quizards have the blue skin. Her blue skin says that she has a blue heart. You are her parents, and you must turn on the light in her blue heart. The three of you need to hold hands as you say the chant. So tomorrow morning, all three of you must be here in front of the statues of Jacque and Evangeline." Marie La Vie stressed again the timing of this chant. "Now do you understand?"

They were both overjoyed, but now they understood how this new rare event of a Quizard being born was so special. Their little blue girl was very rare.

"The legend of the Blue Chant, I heard it this way. Both parents of the Quizard, they hold the magic doorknob key. They place the key into the keyhole, and turn it once to the left, saying the chant. When the key is popped out, the blue heart, it lights up! The Blue Chant goes like this."

With this key for our Quizard, we turn to the left,
We unleash the magic of hope and love to be blessed,
Inside the heart, we light the blue light for our child,
Let the magic be for good and let it run wild."

Wizard Antoine and Queen Faustina embraced. How lucky they were to have more magic in the doll land.

"Let's go and look for the doorknob that has the key now, so we can say the Blue Chant in the morning," Antoine said. "I can hover into the tree tonight and search every inch of the big tree. My shoes still allow me to hover above ground. As far as I know, I don't have a time limit on the magic of my shoes."

"GREAT idea!" said Faustina as she started her long stride out the house. "I'll tell the sugar mill ladies to watch the girls while we look in the oak tree. The key has to be in the oak tree. It's the only place I have doorknobs chimes. The Cajun Fairies can help us."

The three of them left the house. It was dark, but they had enough time until morning. The street lamps along the braided rug road left a dim light outside, but the fireflies still lit the way. The big oak tree was full of wind chimes.

"Oh, Mon Gris-Gris!" Marie La Vie said. "There are so many

wind chimes. It has to be one that is a doorknob, and it has to have a key hanging down the middle of the chime. If there is no key, I don't know what to do. We need both."

Marie kept looking up at the huge tree and the vast collection of chimes there were.

"We need more help! Faustina, how many you have? Oh Mon Gris-Gris!"

"I have at least a dozen or more doorknobs, but for the love of Sha Bebe, where do we begin looking?"

Antoine spoke up. "Send the Cajun Fairies to the top of the tree. The fireflies will light up their way. While they look above, you can look below, I'll hover into the middle section."

"GREAT idea," said Faustina as she began looking feverously for any doorknob key chime. "I *think* I have at least a dozen or so of that kind. So, as we find one, let's put it on the ground near the statues of Jacque and Evangeline. This way we can count how many we find." They all agreed.

The search for the magic key had begun.

Clotilda, Matilda and Emelda had made their way through the sugar cane fields to get the new Quizard. Emelda, with her big puffy, black hair, had caught it several times in the sugarcane, but the other two had scissors in their bags to cut the loose ends of the canes out of her hair. They followed her like baby ducklings follow the mother duck.

Emelda looked at Clotilda, "How did you end up with white hair when both of us have hair as black as coal?"

"WHY are you worried about the color of my hair right now?" Clotilda raised her voice. "I don't know! Maybe I look like our mama. She had white hair. Remember. Ever thought about that, Emelda? Shut up, and let's GO."

Matilda looked at Clotilda in shock. Both of them rarely spoke. Emelda was always the boss. The leader. Neither one of them ever spoke back to Emelda!

"Yes, Emelda, she looks like our mama, now let's GO." Matilda spoke up.

"Oh, just because we're on a mission to get some blue doll for Ophelia, you think you can YELL at me?"

"YES," Matilda spoke up again.

"Why?" Emelda was just too curious.

"Because, if we do a good job in getting her this blue doll that she wants so bad, maybe she might start treating us right. You know some people can change!"

"HA!" That was all Emelda could squeak out. "You both crazy!"

"She could change, Emelda. We not as bad as she is. We just took on her bad habits. When we was with mama, we got along good. She changed us, why can't we change her?"

"Ah, just keep moving. We not changing, and Ophelia ain't changing her ways. She was born mean, and she will die mean! Let's GO."

Clotilda and Matilda just hissed and walked behind Emelda. Deep down inside they knew she was right.

Clotilda   Matilda   Emelda

They were at the entrance to the doll land of Sha Bebe,
a place where no human had ever gone before.

Three of the sugar mill ladies were sitting in Queen Faustina's kitchen drinking coffee while the two Princesses were in the next room sound asleep. They could see them very well. The Queen,

Marie La Vie, and the Wizard were outside looking for the doorknob chime with the magic key.

All of a sudden, they heard a noise at the back door and one sugar mill lady got up to open it thinking it was the Queen. It was not. It was the three dwarf sisters!

The sugar mill lady was stunned. Speechless! She was in shock to see a *human*! No human was ever in the doll land. Emelda grabbed her, and put the sleeping snuff under her nose first. The other two ran to protect the two princesses. One tripped over the chair at the table. Emelda got her with the sleeping snuff. The third sugar mill lady ran to the girl's room.

"Two down, one to go. Get the last one before she wakes up the Quizard!" she whispered in that screechy, wavy voice of hers.

Matilda grabbed the third lady and she fell on Molly's bed. Molly woke up as she saw Emelda putting the sleeping snuff under the sugar mill lady's nose.

"Who are you?"

"GRAB her before she wakes up everyone in this land."

As Clotilda grabbed Molly, she screeched, "She's not blue!"

"On the map that we studied for a month, this is the Queen's house. Why are you white and not blue?" Emelda asked Molly, in a frantic voice.

"My sister Maggie is blue." She pointed to the bed next to hers.

"TWO of them! We have to bring two of them?" Emelda was confused and was also in a hurry to get out of there. The plan was not going well. She was supposed to bring Ophelia a blue doll.

"Let's leave the white one here," Clotilda said as she kept a hold on Molly, "and put the sleeping snuff under the blue one's nose. Ophelia doesn't need this white one." She shook her by the arm.

Maggie was still sleeping. They were whispering, but this plan was taking longer than expected. It was supposed to be quick in and out job. And, there was supposed to be one doll, not two.

"We can't leave the white one here!" Emelda was having a quiet hissy fit. "She saw us, and will tell everyone who we are. Then everyone will know, and they will be searching for us, and then Ophelia will be mad at me, and…"

Matilda slapped Emelda across the face! SMACK! "No one knows US! Everyone knows Ophelia. Get a grip, Emelda!"

"That did it." Emelda was furious. "Since when do the both of you tell ME what to do and yell at me? Coming here through the cane field, I let that hair color thing go, but Matilda, you slapped ME?" Her eyes were shining white.

Emelda slapped Matilda back. SMACK … in the face.

"STOP IT!" screeched Clotilda. "Just stop it! You will wake everyone up in this place. Let's take both of them and get out of here. We'll just tell Ophelia what happened. Maybe she can let this one off at Lacey Laurel Lane like the old Quizard." She pulled on Molly's arm while quickly heading for the back door.

"Wait, let me give her some of the sleeping snuff. I don't want her screaming for her mama and daddy." Emelda also spread the sleeping snuff under Maggie's nose, too. "Come on. Let's get out of here!"

She picked up Maggie, threw her over her shoulder and they left for the hole in the dome wall. As they walked quietly under the oak tree, they saw dolls in the oak tree along with some strange looking bug creatures, but they didn't know what they were doing.

"Will you look at this? Up in a tree when it's dark. This doll land has crazy ways." whispered Emelda. The other two agreed by shaking their heads yes as they kept moving through the sugarcane fields until they got to the pirogue.

"Okay." said Emelda, "We made it out of there. We're telling Ophelia that everything went good, without any problems at all. You hear me?" She put the two Princesses on the floor of the pirogue.

Matilda and Clotilda agreed by shaking their heads yes, again. Neither one of them said a word to Emelda. Both of them knew she was furious because Matilda slapped her in the face. They just sat, slumped over, and said nothing.

"Give me that Quizard," said Emelda. She gave them both a look that would have scared the pants off of the dead.

"Each of you take an oar and let's get to the island. Ophelia will have you two in the well with the ghost girl if we get there with no Quizard. I'll blame both of you if anything else goes wrong. Understand?"

Again, they both agreed with a head shake of yes.

"I don't care what happens to the white one, but we'll tell Ophelia that there may be something with this white one to be born with the blue one. We don't know anything about these dolls. They were in a tree at night. Go figure!" She held on to the blue doll tightly. Both of them were passed out cold from the sleeping snuff.

"Huh!" Emelda said in the boat in a low voice mimicking Ophelia. I can just hear her now. *'What do you think I do all day? Look in my mirrors that are splattered all over the house? You are nothing but low life fools. GET me my new Quizard, now! I have work to do.'...* "We do all of her dirty work. She never does any work!"

"You talking to us, Emelda?" Matilda asked.

"No, just keep going to the island. I'm talking to myself."

Chapter 6

Looking for Maggie and Molly

At the altar of Jacque and Evangeline, Wizard Antoine, Queen Faustina and Marie La Vie counted the doorknob chimes. They had sixteen. More than Faustina thought she had. Some had keys, and some did not. They lined them in a row and picked the ones with keys still attached and that pile added up to seven.

"The magic key should be from these seven. There is no key on the rest of the doorknobs. Maggie would not have come to you both without the magic key. If one of the seven do not light her blue heart, we need to find the key. The right key is here. Somewhere." Marie La Vie looked around, but was confident that they had the magical doorknob.

"So, you're sure it's one of these seven?" Queen Faustina had the biggest grin on her face, as she held Antoine's arm, but she had a doubt. She would never go against Marie La Vie's advice, but she wondered why she was doubting her words. That never happened before.

"Yes, I am sure. Tomorrow morning, we do the Blue Chant. We see which doorknob is going to light the blue heart of Maggie. Right there in front of the statues."

"I can't wait," said Faustina. "We will have more festivals and more fun coming to the doll land of Sha Bebe with another doll who can perform magic. This is so exciting!" Faustina rubbed her two hands together with delight and then hugged Antoine.

They headed back to their homes.

Marie La Vie was getting in her pirogue to get back to her swamp shack behind Plume's house, when she heard a terrible scream! "Oh Mon Gris-Gris! Such a frightful yell."

The Cajun Fairies who were helping to find the magic key in the oak tree came flying in the door. They stayed hovering at the door. Shocked at what they saw.

Marie La Vie ran back to the Queen's house. When she ran into the living room she saw three sugar mill ladies on the floor. The Queen was still screaming that the girls were gone. Antoine was running in the back yard looking around every bush and flower plant calling for Maggie and Molly. The Cajun Fairies were still hovering at the door.

"Oh Mon Gris Gris! What happened to the sugar mill ladies?"

"The girls are not in their rooms, and the sugar mill ladies have passed out! Something bad happened here. All three of the ladies are on the floor? I don't like this, and the girls are gone!" The Queen was frantic.

"I can't find the girls!" Antoine told the Queen as he came back into the house. He was out of breath from running and calling their names.

Marie La Vie revived the three sugar mill ladies with her rose water, and helped them to a chair at the kitchen table. Her rose water worked miracles. The Queen got some cold water for them. They sat at the table and talked. They never did speak much, but now, they had word, on top of word, spilling out of their mouths. Never before had anyone in the land heard them speak so fast. They were always quiet ladies who did their cooking and cleaning. But now, they could not stop talking.

With all three speaking at once, the Queen heard the word human. She heard them say that three small humans were at her back door, and she froze.

"*Humans*? Humans in the land of Sha Bebe?" Antoine spoke up.

The Queen was astounded at the word *humans*. More than one entered the land. She was right about her antsy feeling she had before the wedding. Something horrible happened. At that moment she knew the girls were taken by humans. But why?

"Antoine, how could any human get into the doll land? The invisible dome over us has always been solid for our protection. For the love of Sha Bebe, what is going on here?" Now, the Queen was pacing the floor.

"Did these *humans* say their names?" she asked the three

talkative sugar mill ladies. The Queen was waiting for the name Ophelia. The fear of the name Ophelia popped into her mind again.

"No," said the most talkative sugar mill lady who answered the door, "they swarmed into the room and put a smell under our nose. We tried to stop them from going into Maggie and Molly's room, but the smell. Oh that smell made us fall to the floor!"

"Sleeping snuff!" said Marie La Vie. "They used sleeping snuff. That powder will make anyone fall to the floor. Oh, this is no good." She was shaking her head and began pacing the floor with the Queen. Back and forth. Back and forth.

"I did hear one human say, *'Two down and one to go. Get her before she wakes up the Quizard.'* She was talking about me as I was trying to reach the beds of the girls. Her voice sounded like someone was speaking in a fan. It sounded wavy. Then they must have got me too. I don't remember anything else!" She was crying.

Madame Plume and Madame Poulette ran into the house. "We heard a scream. What happened?"

"Oh, Plume, humans entered the land and took Maggie and Molly. Small humans!" The Queen was still pacing the floor alongside of Marie La Vie. Now it was synchronized pacing.

"What! HOW? Antoine, how did humans enter the doll land?" Madame Plume was immediately shocked about the humans and could not stop talking. Madame Poulette was speechless.

Acadia and Olivia, the Cajun Fairies, flew to the Queen and sat on her shoulder. "When we left the doll land to go to Lacey Laurel Lane to get your pink silk flowers, we saw three small humans paddling a pirogue. We hid the fairy boat in an abandoned eagle nest on the old rail car track, and they had the same voices, Faustina. Not quite like our squeaky voices, but they did sound wavy."

"No! Did you hear the name Ophelia?"

Acadia told her yes. "She did say that Ophelia was going to make them do her dirty work, and they couldn't wait to get their hands on the Quizard. But we didn't know what they were talking about! Oh my, if we would have known, we could have warned you and Antoine!" Acadia bowed her head in sorrow. So did Olivia.

"Now, now. How were you supposing to know? This is not your fault. None of us knew about a Quizard until today. It's okay. It's okay." She held the two Cajun Fairies and cuddled them lightly so she wouldn't break their gossamer wings.

Marie La Vie stopped pacing and stood up as stiff as a board. "Ophelia? The three small humans are with Ophelia? OH mon Gris-Gris! Ophelia is human, too! She is not a good human. NO! No good at all!"

Madame Plume sat down on a chair. "Well, I'm so confused

right now I could spit feathers! What is going on here?"

Madame Poulette was totally confused also and told the sugar mill ladies to go back to the kitchen house and to make a big pot of hot tea. They would all need some. She sat down next to Madame Plume at the table.

"If this don't beat all! Antoine, can someone please tell us what is going on here." Madame Plume was flustered. Her hair was in a mess of curls in her face, because she was getting ready for bed. She was rushed all day long with a wedding, and then she was rushed with the birth of not one but two dolls, one being called a Quizard which she had never heard of before. She stood up with her hands on her hips looking at Queen Faustina, the Cajun Fairies, her brother Wizard Antoine, and Marie La Vie. She was breathing heavy and giving all of them the squint eyes.

"Where are the Princesses?" Madame Plume was not mad; she was just very confused. Madame Poulette was still in shock.

Queen Faustina walked over to both of them.

"Okay! Plume and Poulette, listen well. Three small humans, not one, not two, but THREE small humans, came into this house and took both of the girls. They TOOK them! They are gone. POOF. Do you understand that? The name Ophelia just came up, and Marie La Vie said she's no good! I don't know more than that right now either, and if you think for one minute that I will let this Ophelia *human* take my girls and ..."

The Queen was getting upset with Plume, but Plume and Poulette didn't know about the key and how it had to be turned to the Blue Chant ...about the blue heart of a Quizard ...about how rare she was. They didn't know anything!

Marie La Vie stepped in to calm down the Queen. She explained everything to them while the sugar mill ladies brought over a big pot of hot tea. Everyone sat at the table to let this horrible news sink in for a good while. Then, they asked question after question. Marie La Vie answered all of their questions calmly about how she knew a *human* named Ophelia when she lived as a human in New Orleans. She told them how she was a mean, wealthy, spoiled brat, who would do anything to get what she wanted, but she didn't know why she wanted Maggie.

Queen Faustina apologized. "Plume and Poulette, I'm so sorry I was rude to the both of you when you didn't know anything at all about what is going on here. Please forgive me. I'm so upset. The girls were taken away from the land!" She cried.

"That's okay. I shouldn't have been so blunt. I need to stop doing that. Poulette was fine with her manners. I'll learn to stop doing that." She put her head down, because she was embarrassed.

A solemn quiet filled the room for what seemed like an eternity.

Madame Poulette got up and cried with the Queen. "We are so sorry this happened. How can we help? We'll find this Ophelia *human* with you!"

"Help you! Yes, we'll help you. How can we help you and Antoine get those vagabonds?" Madame Plume hugged the Queen but had no tears at all. They were all accustomed to having tears now.

Madame Plume thought to herself as she began pacing the floor. "I'm sad. I can't cry. Why is this happening again?"

In the beginning there were no feelings of sorrow and sadness in the doll land. No tears. It was always a happy place with fun things to do, but horrible events began happening in the doll land that had to be solved. Was this a sign of the times? No trouble ever came their way for centuries. Now about every decade or so, they had problems to solve.

The first time Madame Plume cried, she said her eyes were leaking. She didn't know the word tears, because no one ever was sad. She was getting angry, and yet she felt deeply saddened that her nieces were gone. Not a good feeling for the one who owned the most powerful magic wand in all the doll lands.

"Antoine, let's get everyone in the land together and search around to see if they're not playing outside. You know they could be playing. They don't know all of the rules yet in the land. They just got here today!" Madame Plume had mixed emotions.

"I did look around the land. They're not here. I called their names and no one answered. They're not here, Plume! They have been taken away from us by bad *humans*!"

"Well, we can't just sit here. Now that we all know about how a Quizard's blue heart works with a magical key and that blue chant thing, let's go and find Maggie and Molly. Come on, let's go! I made those girls today, and they come from my wand, and no bad *human* is going to come into this land and take away my precious nieces." Her voice was getting shaky. "And then to top it all off, *humans* just *walk* in here?" Her hands were flying in all directions. "Antoine, shoot some lightning bolts out of your hands or something!"

Madame Plume was losing control.

"Did anyone look around here to see how *humans* got into the land? There is an invisible dome around this place that's supposed to protect us, you know. Why would anyone take Maggie and Molly in the first place? How did they know about a Quizard being rare? When I get my hands on those humans, my wand will turn them into a …

Madame Plume began crying uncontrollably.

Marie La Vie hugged Plume. Tight. "Everything will be okay. Cry all you want. Let it out. We find the girls. Yes, we find them both."

Antoine took control. "Everyone, listen to me. Plume is right. The first thing we need to do is search every inch of this land to find out how humans got inside. Let's wake up everyone and search every inch of the land, right now."

Everyone got out of the Queen's house and rang a big bell to wake up everyone else in the doll land. They all came running outside. Standing on the braided rug road were 100 boys and girls in their pajamas, sixteen sugar mill ladies in bed robes, Miss Betty Lou in her violet night gown, and at least 20 Cajun Fairies were hovering overhead. Marie La Vie, the Queen, the Wizard, Madame Plume, and Madame Poulette were waiting to hear what Wizard Antoine had to say.

"I have sad news. Maggie and Molly are not in this land anymore."

Everyone gasped.

"We all know that three small humans took both of them. I think it's safe to say they won't be back for any of us. They came for a Quizard and took both of them." Antoine's voice was getting angry. He did have a temper, but he needed to stay focused.

He continued. "We will form a tight circle right here in the middle of the braided rug road, and go forward until we all reach the invisible wall. When we get to the invisible dome wall, we will look and feel every inch of the wall at the bottom to see if there is a crack in the wall. Cajun Fairies, you fly high and search the top of the wall. When anyone finds the place that is cracked, they need to yell out that they found it and stay right at that spot. I'll be right there. Let's begin."

Everyone walked to the wall and did exactly as Antoine said. It didn't take long until one of the boys found a hole in the wall. He yelled, and Antoine ran right over to where he heard the yell. Marie La Vie, Madame Plume and the Queen followed.

Once again, they all gasped, and Marie La Vie said, "OH Mon Gris-Gris!" How? How did this happen?"

Antoine told everyone to stand back and the lightning bolts from his hands melted the hole in the wall back together. Then he told everyone to go back into their houses while he reinforced the entire dome. When all of them were inside, Antoine, with a rage in his eyes that could have melted the whole doll land, focused his attention on the invisible dome. Lightning bolts were shooting onto every inch of the dome. The color of the dome stayed crystal clear, but it was reinforced. No human had ever penetrated the wall. Only the dolls could go in and out the land at will. There were no boundaries for them, and they saw no invisible dome.

Antoine ran back to the Queen's house with Madame Plume, Madame Poulette and Marie La Vie. The Cajun Fairies stayed in the room and ate the grapes that were on the table.

"I'm satisfied with the strength of the wall, but what do we do now? None of us know where this Ophelia human is or this island. How will we find Maggie and Molly?"

Acadia landed on Faustina's shoulder again. In her squeaky voice she said, "We saw the small humans at Lacey Laurel Lane. Why not begin the search there?"

"Really! What were they doing in that land of dolls? Only dolls can get in there through the lantern portal pole. That's strange!"

"We don't know, but they were following us everywhere we went. We saw their human fingers. If we had known, we could have warned you." Acadia felt sad again.

"Now, I've told you and Olivia already that you had no idea what was going on. None of us did. Until now. Don't be sad about that. You've given us good information." The Queen gently hugged Acadia.

Olivia flew onto the Queen's shoulder and spoke up. "When we were coming home with the silk flowers, I heard one small human say they needed to get back to the island as fast as they could, because Ophelia would be angry with them. When we were at Lacey Laurel Lane, I flew to the end of the lanes and there is a bayou at the end of the lanes. Maybe they got in that doll land by way of that bayou. I did see an island far away in the distance from that bayou, but I don't know how to get there with the fairy boat. Maybe that's the island! We could fly there and see who lives on that island."

"Great idea!" The Queen was overjoyed at this good news.

Poulette jumped up! "I have a plan. I - have - a - plan!" She slapped her hands together. "It can work! The fairies don't know what bayou is behind Lacey Laurel Lane. None of us do, but we all know how to get *to* Lacey Laurel Lane. Let's all go on a magic quilt ride --- and go there. Then we can go to the bayou in the back and see the island. It's a brilliant plan!" Now *she* was pacing the floor. Thinking and pacing.

"I can zap five large magic flying quilts with my magic wand. One quilt for each of us. I can do that right now. It won't take me long. The Cajun Fairies can ride with Marie until we find out how far this island is from Lacey Laurel Lane, and then they can fly on their own to see what the place on the island looks like. We'll be in a place we know nothing about. The Cajun Fairies are tiny and they can sneak around over the island and not be seen. If we go straight to the house, we'll be in plain view and whoever lives there will see us."

Madame Plume snickered, "And how do you think we will we get into Lacey Laurel Lane? We can't all fit in that lantern portal pole, you know!" She was shaking her head as if she didn't agree with the plan at all.

"Listen to me, Plume! You know I have a good plan. It will work, and we can take each a turn going into the lantern portal pole. How hard would that be? Not hard at all. You're the one who's not thinking?"

"I AM thinking, Poulette! Boy, you are something else. You think we can just all fly over Lacey Laurel Lane with all of those fancy porcelain dolls in their satin, Victorian dresses, and their big fancy bonnets and umbrellas, just looking up at us cloth dolls dressed in rag wear? Just gawking at us! You know how snobby they are to any rag dolls. No matter what we wear. And we'll be on quilts! HA. We'll be laughed at."

"Stop it, Plume! Who cares what those snobby porcelain dolls think about rag dolls? We can get in, and we can find that island from Lacey Laurel Lane. You just jealous because you didn't think about this plan first. I'm telling you it will work, and when we get there…"

The Queen's head was moving back and forth listening to

each of them raising their voice at each other. Antoine and Marie La Vie were doing the same thing. It was like watching the ball on a ping pong table go back and forth.

"Whoa. Wait one minute here!" The Queen interrupted. "Are you both forgetting about Maggie and Molly? Time is running out for us to do the turning of the key ritual and the Blue Chant. Stop it!"

Marie La Vie slide in between Plume and Poulette, and in a soft voice said, "I think Poulette's plan is excellent. I take over from here." She looked at Queen Faustian and Wizard Antoine and sent them a wink.

"Plume your part in the plan will be using your magic wand. After all, you have the most powerful magic wand of all the wands. You be there to protect us with anything that comes out of the wand if we need protection. Your wand protected us from the Ugly Babies. Remember? Ophelia has no power, but she is very evil and makes potions and things that hurt the humans. Maybe dolls too."

Marie held the mole between her eyes, because she had a faint tingle. Her mole, which she called her third eye, was very sensitive to negative energy and feelings. "I have not been around Ophelia since I left New Orleans to move here. I do not know what she can do, but we need your wand. I feel there will be much trouble from her."

Madame Plume looked at Madame Poulette and sent her a sly

smile, like she was important.

Marie La Vie turned to Madame Poulette. "Poulette, you will need to go and get those big, magic flying quilts so we can make the way to Lacey Laurel Lane. We cannot get there any other way. We have until 3:33 pm tomorrow to get Maggie and Molly back to here, or Maggie loses the magic that comes to her. We cannot forget the timing in this. Both of you have important things to do."

They both smiled and felt as though they really were going to help in some way. Both of them felt needed, and it was a good feeling inside.

Marie La Vie thought about what she said. "Huh, we never bother with time in the doll land the way the humans do, and now we need to watch time. Strange."

"Antoine can use his pocket watch that his dad gave him so we can keep track of human time." Poulette shook her head at Plume and gave her one of her -- '*I won*' -- looks.

"Good for you, Poulette. Antoine will bring his pocket watch."

Queen Faustina and Wizard Antoine were ready.

"It's almost morning and none of us had any rest. We need to get things ready to leave. We'll do as Marie La Vie said. Antoine has his watch, but he will set it to human time when we get to Lacey

Laurel Lane. We really have no time to waste."

Marie La Vie said, "There is that word again. TIME.

Chapter 7

Through the Portal into Lacey Laurel Lane

Everyone had only a few hours to rest and eat before heading out to Lacey Laurel Lane to find Princess Maggie and Princess Molly, but they were ready for the journey. Madame Poulette had the five big magic flying quilts. Madame Plume was ready with her magic wand in her hand.

The sugar mill ladies assured the Queen that they would keep everything in order in the doll land while they were gone, now that they knew no human could enter since Antoine reinforced the invisible dome. There would a feast for the Princesses when they returned. The kitchen would be filled with good food and lots of cakes and pastries. The Bebe Land Band told Wizard Antoine that they would be playing some good, loud music to welcome everyone home.

Miss Betty Lou would stay with the 100 boys and girls. She assured them that she was okay, but was so saddened that Maggie and Molly were missing. She bid them a quick, 'I hope they will be home soon', took out her handkerchief to wipe her tears, and went back into the school house.

With five large magic quilts laid out on the braided rug road, Madame Poulette tapped each one of them and off they flew into the sky not knowing where they would end up. Destination unknown, but that island couldn't be too far away. Madame Poulette was the last one to fly out, and her view of the quilts in the sky gave her much pride in knowing that she was helping with this mission in a big way. This time they would have to face up to a human. A bad *human*!

Marie La Vie led the way with the Cajun Fairies telling her how to get to the lantern portal pole to enter Lacey Laurel Lane. When they landed in the court yard each one folded their flying quilts and tucked it under their arms. The two Cajun Fairies went into the lantern portal pole first with Marie La Vie. The Queen, Madame Poulette, and Madame Plume took each a turn to enter with Wizard Antoine going in last. When they got to the big iron gate, they passed through it with no problems.

"Okay, what now?" asked Plume. "Do we walk along the lanes or fly over head? I don't want to see even one of those snooty porcelain dolls give me any kind of *look* at all, or I will …"

"For the love of Sha Bebe, will you stop worrying about the porcelains, Plume? What is wrong with you these days? We're on a mission to find our two Princesses. Get yourself in a better mood or get back on your flying quilt and go back to the doll land."

"Faustina, I'm sorry. I don't know what's happening to me lately, but it's ever since my wand POPPED Molly out on its own. When I saw her, I knew I didn't do that. I feel the same as you did for the wedding. Something bad is coming and I don't know what it is."

Plume was about to cry. The Queen held her tightly and told her not to worry.

"Look at me Plume. You did a wonderful job with your magic wand bringing a Quizard into the land. None of us even knew anything about a Quizard, except Marie."

Marie La Vie bowed her head.

"So, worrying about the porcelain dolls should be the last thing on your mind right now. Let's go and find Maggie and Molly."

Madame Plume knew the Queen was right.

"I think we must fly over this Lacey Laurel Lane," said Marie La Vie. "This way we can see the island the way the fairies saw the island. We can't waste time walking the circle roads!"

The Queen agreed. There was no time for walking around the circles of lanes. So each of them got back on the quilts and took off into the air after Poulette gave each one of the quilts a tap with her magic wand.

Plume was right though about the dolls gawking at them. Every doll below was watching the flying quilts overhead. It wasn't only the porcelain dolls, but it was every doll walking and shopping along the lanes. Many got out of the shops to see what the talking was all about. All of them were saying loudly, "LOOK up there. WOW. What is that? Who are those dolls?"

All of a sudden, Plume felt special. She began waving to all of the dolls below, and they waved back to her. "Faustina, they like us! All of the dolls like us. Look they are waving to all of us."

"Yes, I see that, Plume. Dolls are much nicer than humans."

Plume swooped down low with her quilt and began zigzagging left and right slowly. "Hi, were from a magical doll land called Sha Bebe. The Queen is flying up there. She got married to the Wizard today, and he's my brother."

She was holding on to the front of her flying quilt, driving it like it was one of those cars for a human. She didn't know if the dolls could hear her well, but she kept making tricks with her quilt and showing off.

Madame Poulette had never seen her fly on her quilt like that before. "PLUME, stop clowning around with the quilt. You'll run into a tree! You're flying very low now. STOP IT!"

She loved attention, but this wasn't the time to be playing around.

"Poulette, I know what I'm doing!" Madame Plume was a little annoyed that Poulette fussed her. "I'm keeping up with all of you. Don't worry about me, I'm right behind all of you! You watch where you're going."

The minute Madame Plume said that to Madame Poulette, her

quilt slammed right into a wooden lamp pole. BOOM! It knocked her out cold. All of them quickly turned around their flying quilts to help Plume. The dolls in Lacey Laurel Lane were all around Madame Plume asking her if she was okay. They were fascinated with her dress full of feathers.

Madame Poulette slid in on the sidewalk with her quilt. "Plume, are you okay? Move. Please move. My best friend is hurt! Oh Sha, are you okay?"

One of the porcelain dolls was a nurse and got her up and walking.

"What happened to me?" Madame Plume was dazed.

The porcelain doll nurse told her that she would be okay as she kept putting a cold towel on her head. She had dolls all around her who she didn't know, but she finally saw Madame Poulette.

"Poulette?" You could see she wanted to cry.

"Well, you did it again. You ran straight into the wooden pole lamp on the street in Lacey Laurel Lane. I told you to slow down and stop making fancy spins with the quilt. But no. You had to show off. You are always showing off! Are you okay, Sha?"

"I think I'm okay. I have no bones to break, but I lost a few feathers on my dress."

Poulette helped her get the flying quilt, but it was torn. Just ripped to pieces.

"How fast were you going?"

"Not fast at all," Madame Plume said, still feeling dazed. "Are we on the island where Ophelia lives yet?"

When the dolls of Lacey Laurel Lane heard her say that, all of them backed away from her. They began mumbling amongst themselves.

The Queen saw what happened at the mention of Ophelia's name and had to ask. "Do any of you know who this person named Ophelia is? She took my twin girls, but one is a rare Quizard. She's a blue doll, and we're on a journey to find Ophelia's house and take my twin girls back from her!"

A man doll moved up, dressed in Scottish kilts, with a black Scottish terrier on a leash. In an accent they never heard before he said, "I saw a blue doll hanging around here, but I don't know if she ever goes home. She sleeps on the sidewalk near the hat shop, and in the morning just roams around. I saw her eating food from the trash bin over there. Odd behavior, I thought."

"Do you know where she is now?" the Queen asked.

"Usually at the hat shop, two shops down. She doesn't speak much, and she's no bother to anyone, but she may be your blue doll."

All of them got their quilts and walked over to the hat shop except Madame Plume. She was making friends with every doll in Lacey Laurel Lane. She now loved the porcelain dolls.

The Queen entered the hat shop. "Hello. Have you seen a blue doll hanging around here?"

The nice lady answered, "Yes, I tried to get her to come and stay with me, but she seems shy. I think someone just dropped her off at Lacey Laurel Lane. She's not far from here if you walk along this road. She has a pink dress on. I don't know her name."

"Thank you so much, but that doesn't sound like my Maggie. My Maggie would have talked to you and she would have told you her name. She's not shy at all."

Antoine, Marie La Vie and Madame Poulette were standing outside the hat shop at the open door when Poulette saw a blue doll slip in between the hat shop and wig shop.

"Hey, little blue doll! Please don't go away. Talk to me."

When Faustina exited the hat shop she heard Madame Poulette call the blue doll. "Really Poulette. Did you see her? Where is she? I need to see her!"

"Right here, Faustina. She's afraid or shy. I don't know what it is, but she's hiding right here!" Madame Poulette felt so sad for her.

Queen Faustina went to her and softly said, "Hi. I don't know your name, but I have a little blue doll by the name of Maggie. She wasn't dressed like you but she has a blue skin, just like you do."

She smiled and touched her hands. "And, she is just as pretty as you are too!" She kept comforting the girl. "Do you know that the lady in the hat shop would want you to live with her? If you don't know that, she does. She just told me."

Faustina was now hugging the little blue doll. "What's your name?"

"I don't remember my name. Ophelia had me for so long, and never called me a name. She just touched my blue skin every day. She was born ugly, and when she touched my skin, she became beautiful. I was living with a nice old man in Hawaii, and she took me away from him. She was mean to me." She began to cry.

Marie La Vie was listening to every word that the blue doll and Queen Faustina were saying.

"Well, you won't need to worry about that mean lady ever again. I'm a Queen from a magical doll land who's looking for my own little blue doll who came to me just today. Can you tell me if this lady Ophelia has my little blue girl doll?"

"No, but I heard her tell the three dwarf sisters who live with her to go and get a blue doll."

"Really! Do you think she has my little blue girl doll now?"

"Yes, because she sent Emelda to drop me off here. I can't help Ophelia anymore. My blue skin kept her beautiful. That was my magic power. But now that my skin is no longer working, she got rid of me. She's not a nice lady at all. I don't want to go back with her!" She began to cry again.

"Oh no, no. You will stay right here with the lady in the hat shop. She said that she wanted a little blue girl just like you." Queen Faustina lovingly pinched her little cheeks and brought her into the hat shop. The shop lady was thrilled to have a blue doll. She would help her and bring her lots of business. No one had seen a blue doll before, and the hat lady loved her from the minute she laid eyes on her.

Poulette was crying. "Such a touching thing for the hat lady to do. Now they can both help each other and the little girl now has a good place to live."

Faustina looked at Antoine. "I think we may have more trouble getting the girls than we ever thought. This Ophelia lady is mean. Did you hear what the little Quizard girl said?"

"I heard the whole story, and I'm ready to get Maggie and Molly. It makes me no difference how mean she is. We wasted time here. We need to leave."

Antoine went over the Madame Plume to tell her that she

would be riding with Poulette, because her quilt was torn to shreds.

"Antoine, these are my new friends. I was telling them all about our magical land."

"Hello. I don't mean to be rude, but we need to leave now to get to Ophelia's house. We know our twins, Maggie and Molly, are there."

One of Plume's new friends said, "Ophelia Amedee? Oh my! She's evil. So evil. No one here in Lacey Laurel Lane or in human land want to be near her. We hope you get your girls back, soon."

Plume answered, "Oh, she's not our friend. She took my nieces and we're going to get them back. This is my brother Antoine. He's a Wizard, and the dad of the twin girls I was telling you about. Both dolls were popped to life by my wand." Plume smiled.

"You may need more than your magic wand to deal with Ophelia. She's ruthless!"

Antoine asked, "Exactly where does she live. Do you know?"

"Oh yes. She lives far across the bayou in the back of Lacey Laurel Lane. If you use your wonderful flying quilts, you can get to her house. But I don't know what she will do if she sees all of you coming. She moved from the city to live alone because no one liked her at all. We all know of her, but she's not allowed in here. She's a *human*."

"Yes, we know." Antoine tipped his hat to the lady who told him where she lived and said thank you. All of them gathered their things, and said good bye. Madame Plume assured all of them she would return.

Marie La Vie pulled the Queen and Antoine aside before they left. "We will need a plan to get near the island and into the house. Let's ride until we see trees and think up something to get the girls. From everything I hear, Ophelia didn't change in no way. I don't know what she can do today. Let's go now."

Chapter 8

Finding Dr. Ophelia Amedee

The trip across the bayou was long. It was more like the size of a lake than a bayou. The Queen was very quiet sitting on her quilt wondering how all of this was going to turn out, and if she was going to get her girls back. Plume and Poulette were ready with their magic wands, although Poulette didn't know what her wand would be any good for. All the wand did was make the magic flying quilts and perform the dance of the flying plates.

Marie La Vie had her powerful rose water. Antoine had fire in his eyes and was more than ready to shoot lightning bolts from his hands to get his Princesses back home. The Cajun Fairies were going to do anything they could to help by spying around the house on the small island. All they needed to do was not let Ophelia see them coming to her private island as the dolls from Lacey Laurel Lane warned them.

They saw the house. There were no trees to hide in near the island. The only trees in sight were on the island near the house, and they didn't want to get that close yet. Everyone hovered in midair on their flying quilts over the water. There was nowhere to hide. Water surrounded the entire island

"Now what?" Plume said with an attitude. "We're stuck in midair with no place to hide. You know how I feel antsy when I think we're lost or have no plan! What will we do? How will we get there by at *least* 3:00 pm?" Now she was getting afraid. "Antoine what time do you have on your pocket watch? Oh my goodness, I think I'm going to faint. I have no…"

"Plume calm down and lower your voice! It's so quiet here, they might hear you!"

"OH, we're far from the house, they can't hear me but we have no place to hide and we're lost!" Her chin was quivering. She wanted to cry.

"We're not lost, and it's 2:30. We only have one more hour left, because we had to make that stop at Lacey Laurel Lane," he gave her the squint eyes. "We don't have much human time left. I don't like watching *time*," Antoine answered in a frustrated voice.

"I'm sorry Antoine, but something came over me when I saw all of the porcelain dolls and I just started showing off. I'm sorry!"

Madame Plume didn't like feeling lost. Being on the same quilt with Madame Poulette, she tried help her antsy feeling. "Plume, everything happens for a reason. After you were knocked out cold running into that wooden pole at Lacey Laurel Lane, we got a lot of information for the dolls there. We lost some time, but we know more about Ophelia now. So you see…"

Marie La Vie interrupted. "Plume, can your wand make a tree?"

"What?"

"A tree. Can your wand make a tree?"

"A tree! I never thought about making a tree before," she giggled. "My magic wand can make my dolls come to life, mostly. But it threw that green foam at the Ugly Babies! Remember that?"

"Yes, I remember." Marie La Vie looked at Antoine and winked.

"Yes, and that helped us defeat those ugly dolls who were so mean on that horrible day. I didn't even know my wand could do that." she shrugged her shoulders as she looked around at nothing in midair.

"My wand made a Quizard come alive today... and Molly!" she smiled at Marie La Vie.

"So... if your wand can make things come to life, why can't it make a tree come to life from the water so we can sit in that tree and hide from Ophelia?"

"I don't know that answer. I never made a tree before."

Madame Plume was thinking that Marie La Vie was making a lot of sense. Her wand brought things to life. She already knew that her wand could end a life too, but that was only to be done in self-defense or to help someone in danger. Marie had always warned her not to cross 'the line of ending'. If she did that, she would pay dearly for taking a life. How she would pay, Marie didn't know, so she warned her to never do that without knowing in her heart that she was doing the right thing. But Plume loved her wand and giving life. It's what she lived for.

"Plume," Marie continued, "if your wand could pop a big tree over there in the water, we would be close enough to see the house, and to hide to make a plan to get in that house and get Maggie and Molly."

"I can try. My wand brings life. There is life in a tree, and we need a big, beautiful tree." Now Plume felt safer, and she knew they needed someplace to hide. "I'll try it!"

Everyone was overjoyed in a quiet way. There was an eerie silence over the water. No boat traffic at all.

Madame Plume stood up on her quilt. Madame Poulette held her dress so the quilt wouldn't tilt to one side and she pointed to the spot where Marie La Vie told her to POP a tree. She did exactly what she would do when she popped a doll to life. There were no fabrics flying around, but low and behold, a tree began growing from the water. Slowly.

Low whispers of cheers were said by the five of them and everyone was hoping no one in the house could see a tree growing. It was growing at a slow but steady pace, not too far from the island, but as the tree got taller and fuller, they heard no noise, no one screaming, nothing was coming from that old house of Ophelia.

Madame Plume was jumping on the quilt, and almost threw Madame Poulette off.

"Plume, calm down. We'll both fall into the water. Oh Sha, you did well. That is the most beautiful tree I've ever seen. You did it."

"It is a beautiful tree!" Plume felt so much pride in what she did to help. "I didn't know my wand could POP a tree, but it did!

"For sure!" said Marie La Vie. "Now, let's fly to the tree at the back side, and we hope no one sees us."

The Queen and Wizard Antoine lead the way. "We lost some more time, but Plume that was good what you did. I'm proud to call you my sister."

Madame Plume felt she redeemed herself for the blunder that happened at Lacey Laurel Lane.

They got to the tree with no one seeing them. Everyone picked a different brand to lay their quilt on. Now they listened for voices. They heard nothing. The Queen began thinking about Princess Maggie and Molly. How were they being treated? What did they eat? Did Ophelia treat them well? So many questions were going through her mind.

Antoine, on the other hand, wanted to hover over the house and break into the house. His rage had been building up since the time he couldn't find them in the yard in the doll land. But he didn't know if he would put Maggie and Molly in danger by doing that. So they sat and observed for a few minutes.

"Antoine, what time is it now?"

"It's only 15 minutes before 3:00 pm, Plume. We won't have enough time. Maggie will lose her magic before we get back to the doll land, but she's still our Maggie. We're bringing both of them home. Magic or no magic."

"Oh, Antoine, I'm so sorry. Maybe if I had not acted like show off at Lacey Laurel Lane, we would have made it here on time."

"Not to worry about time now," said Marie La Vie. "Everything is as it is. We get Maggie and Molly."

I don't know how the humans make it watching *time*. It's just not right watching a pocket watch instead of doing other things." Antoine's voice was drained. "If this feeling is worry, I don't like it."

Marie La Vie said, "Yes, this is worry."

She thought about her spiritual altar at her swamp shack behind Madame Plume's house. She wished she was back at her home and there would be no worry, but she knew there was big trouble coming. She took some of powerful rose water out of her pocket and secretly sprinkled the Queen and the Wizard to ease their worry.

Marie La Vie at her altar in her swamp shack.

Chapter 9

The Rescue

Meanwhile, in Ophelia's house, she was having a hissy fit because she had two dolls instead of one. Emelda knew she would be mad at that, but she explained how they had to bring both of them to her. The white one had seen them in the Queen's house.

"I know what you said to me Emelda, but now I have two of them, and I don't want the white doll!" she screamed and threw a vase at the wall with all of her strength. It shattered into a hundred pieces.

Matilda and Clotilda were shaking while they listened in the next room.

"I just got rid of the other blue one. I hate dolls! They creep me out! Slimy little things that look at you with glazed, creepy eyes that stare. They just sit and stare. They never DO anything. But these dolls TALK! They even have a heart that beats. Who ever heard of such a thing about dolls?"

Ophelia grabbed Molly by the arm. "Here, take this one and put her in the room upstairs. I don't care what happens to her. I only want the blue doll!"

Molly was not afraid. She broke loose of Ophelia's grip, ran to Maggie and said, "I'm not leaving my twin sister here with you! I'm staying with her."

"Excuse me! No one tells me what to do! Who are you to tell

me what to do?" Ophelia's arms were flying all over the place. "And why is your *twin* sister blue? Twins are supposed to look the same."

Ophelia had fire in her eyes that could have lit up every bon fire on the levee in New Orleans on New Year's Eve.

"We're not identical twins, as you can see, but I came here to protect my sister Maggie, and that's what I will do. We stay together!" She stomped her foot on the floor and had one hand on her hip. "Where she goes, I go!"

"Get a load of this one Emelda. She will tell me what she wants." Ophelia was laughing uncontrollably. She never laughed. Ever.

Emelda joined Ophelia with a forced laugh out of her mouth while Molly was holding on tight to Maggie's hand, but she had never seen Ophelia this mad before.

"I TELL YOU what to do, and you do it. Understand?"

Molly stomped her foot on the floor again in defiance.

"Cute little foot you have there. Stop stomping your foot on the floor or I will cut it off. I WILL! I will get my scissors and just cut both of your feet OFF!"

Molly stepped back and stood in front of Maggie.

"You are not staying with your sister, dearie, so get over it, now! Emelda will take you in the upstairs room where you will stay until I tell you to get out. It's almost 3:33 pm."

Emelda grabbed Molly and was hauling her up the stairs. Molly was screaming for Maggie. Matilda and Clotilda helped her to get Molly upstairs, but she was just as strong as the three of them put together.

Ophelia circled around Maggie and looked at her. Her face lit up with an impish grin, because she had her new toy. "Come here, blue doll. Let me touch your skin. It's time."

Maggie was shaking. Ophelia touched Maggie's blue skin but she felt nothing. There was no tingle. Not one part of her body felt younger inside. She ran to her mirror and saw that she still looked the same. A closer look in the mirror showed a few wrinkles began to appear on her cheeks. Ophelia immediately went into panic mode.

"Why can't you make me beautiful? I touched your skin. It's 3:33 pm. Why can't I feel anything when I touch your skin like the other blue doll? Tell me!"

"I don't know. I just got here today. I met my mama and daddy, and then I went play outside with the other boys and girls. I'm the only one with a blue skin, but no one else wanted to touch my skin." Maggie's voice was shaking.

She took Maggie's arm and rubbed harder.

"Ouch, you're hurting me. Stop." The more she would tell her to stop, the harder Ophelia rubbed her arm.

"STOP it, you're hurting me!" She began to cry.

Molly could hear Maggie screaming for her as she was still fighting the three dwarf sister up the stairs. "Let my sister go. She said you're hurting her. Let her go!"

Ophelia went ballistic. She picked up another vase to throw, and this one hit one of her precious mirrors. The force of her throw shattered the mirror and the vase.

"Emelda, bring her sister down here!"

It took the three of them to keep a tight hold on Molly coming down the stairs. They threw her with Maggie. Molly immediately got in front of Maggie.

"I don't understand why this blue doll can't make me feel that tingle that the other blue doll made me feel. It's past 3:33 pm, now!" Ophelia was pacing the floor. "And you went and bring the other blue doll to Lacey Laurel Lane, Emelda!"

"You TOLD me to bring her to Lacey Laurel Lane, Ophelia! You need a drink!"

Between Ophelia's loud, deep voice and the dwarf sister's wavy voices, the Princesses let go of their hands and were holding each other in a hug.

"Give me your arm, dearie!" Ophelia grabbed Molly. "Maybe

it's a white doll this time that will give me beauty." They held onto each other, and Ophelia rubbed until there was almost no more cloth left on Molly's arm. Ophelia was worn out rubbing on their arms, and the Princesses were now both crying and screaming.

Cromwell went back into his sarcophagus saying, "What's a mummy to do here? Nothing. I'm dead anyway!"

The ghost girl got out of the well and sat at the door outside to hear what was going on, and the screaming got louder and louder.

"EMELDA, bring me that drink. Bring me the whole bottle of rum. I need to figure out what the problem is here. I don't know what to do. I always get what I want. I'll lose my beauty. It's past 3:33!"

Molly spoke up. "You think that we can bring you beauty. How?"

"You know how and one of you better tell me soon. I saw a few wrinkles coming on my face. The other blue doll kept me young and beautiful. Why can't this blue doll do that?"

"That was the other Quizards magic ways. Every Quizard has different magic bestowed upon them. Maggie must have a different magic than the other blue doll."

"Just great! That's just great. Now, what do I do?" Ophelia went to another mirror and saw more wrinkles appearing on her face.

"GREAT!"

"There's more to life than having beauty, and being young, you old hag!" Molly was fed up with this bully. "You don't know anything about life."

"Hag! You dare to call me an old HAG?"

Emelda went past the radar room and into the living room to get her bottle of rum. As she was passing back through the radar room that Ophelia had spent a fortune to equip to find a Quizard, she looked out the window and saw a huge tree where there was no tree before. She stepped back and stood at that window. "This is new. How can a tree grow so fast near this small island?"

She waddled into the room with the bottle of rum and a glass and told Ophelia about the new tree.

Ophelia took a shot of the rum straight out of the bottle. "This one here, called me a HAG! I'll rip her to pieces!"

"Ophelia! Stop it. Something's wrong! There's a big tree outside where there was no big tree before."

"A new tree? What do you mean there's a new tree? That has nothing to do with the problem I'm having here with this white doll calling me an old HAG!"

"Ophelia, it's a big tree. Trees don't grow like that overnight. Something isn't right! Suppose those live dolls floated a tree near the island to come and get these dolls? There's something wrong I tell you!"

Ophelia took another shot of rum straight from the bottle. Two more shots and she would be stinking drunk, so Emelda took the bottle from her while she was only tipsy and asked her to come and look out the window at the new tree outside.

"Ahhhhh....... A tree! Okay, what tree Emelda? Show me the new tree." Ophelia was focusing to see the tree out of the window.

"I bet it's our daddy who made that tree. He's coming to save us from you!" Molly spoke up and gave Ophelia a dirty look. "He's a Wizard and he has magic powers in his hands. We come from a magical land. Our mama is a Queen. Madame Plume and Madame Poulette have magic wands too."

"Yea. Yea. Yea. Your daddy is a Wizard with magic hands. Well, maybe he can give me beauty. I can give him whatever he wants. I have lots of money."

"We don't need money where we live, and my daddy will not help you. You took us away from them!"

Molly looked at Maggie, "I bet it's our daddy who's here to bring us home. I bet it is!" She was all smiles. Maggie was standing behind Molly.

Ophelia turned away from the window.

"What is this white doll taking about? Saying things like, her daddy is coming to save her. There are magical dolls with magic wands. There's a Queen, a Wizard. What else?" Ophelia hiccupped. "Is there a little fairy who flies around, too?" She laughed loud and was walking sideways towards the girls. Tipsy. It was a good thing that Emelda took the bottle away from her before she got stinking drunk. Now she was chilled out tipsy, but still dangerous.

"Yes, we do have fairies, and they can fly!" Molly pushed Ophelia.

"Girl! You push me! Come outside with me and we'll see if your *daddy* is here," Ophelia staggered to the front door and stepped out on the porch. "Oh, big, bad daddy coming to save his little girls, where are you?" she said sarcastically.

"Emelda, tie the blue doll in my chair and bring me my torch. I'll burn that tree down." She did.

Maggie and Molly were screaming not to burn the tree down, because if their daddy was in the tree, he would be burned, but Emelda came in with a huge torch. The smell of kerosene filled the room.

The three dwarfs were running around not knowing what Emelda would do next. The ghost girl decided to go inside the house to see if she could help, but she thought it was useless. None of them had never seen Ophelia this angry before.

"Come outside on the porch white doll. We'll have ourselves a big bon fire. Your sister's blue skin is no good to me, and I'm doomed." She hiccupped. "So let's have some fun. The game is over. I don't have a Quizard that works." Molly saw Ophelia wanting to cry. Probably for the first time in her life.

"Then take us back to the doll land. Why do you want to be so mean? If neither one of us is any good for you. Take us back."

While Ophelia was fiddling with the box of matches to light the torch, she answered, "Do you know what it feels like to be ugly? No you don't. Miss cutie pie face. It don't feel good at all. People make fun of you, and they laugh at you."

"I was just born today, but if you want people to like you, why don't you be nice to them. Maybe they'll be nice to you." Molly was sincere with her words.

"AH, people aren't nice," said Ophelia as she hiccupped again. "You don't know what you're talking about. Emelda, bring her outside."

When Molly got on the front porch, Ophelia had the torch in one hand, and a big box of matches in the other hand. She kept fumbling around with the big box of matches. Very uncoordinated from the rum.

"If you thinking of running away, go on. I own this whole small island. You can run all around the house, scream, jump, play in the mud, as far as I'm concerned. I don't care what happens to you."

"SEE, that's why no one cares about YOU! Because you don't care about anyone but your own self. Everything is all about YOU! No wonder you led a miserable life!" Molly screamed at her.

"I heard Molly!" said the Queen.

Everyone who was hidden in the huge tree moved branches to see what was going on at the house. Until now, they didn't hear any of the fussing and crying inside. Ophelia was seen for the first time by all of them. They all gasped and Marie La Vie said, "Oh Mon Gris-Gris!"

Antoine was ready! "I'm getting Molly." He held the two ends of his magic flying quilt and headed towards the old house.

"I just got here today," Molly continued. "I never saw you before, and I don't know who you are, but I know this much, it's not because you're ugly that you're miserable. It's because you're mean. Don't you know that people like you if you're kind and nice to them? You should feel that inside of you without anyone telling you that."

Molly was still crying her words out trying to get Ophelia to let her and Maggie go home. All of a sudden, she stopped crying knowing Ophelia would never change. She had a heart made of ice, and no one can hug a block of ice.

"I came here with no fear in my heart, and I'm here to protect Maggie." "That's my purpose. You treat your three friends in there like slaves. You have no purpose in your life and you are a sour human! Just like rotten fruit that falls from a tree." Molly was talking very fast. "You make them bring everything for you. Can't you do anything for yourself? Don't you have any compassion?"

"Just shut up and go play." She hiccupped while she was still fiddling with the matches. Every time she opened the box, most of the matches would fall on the porch. Getting annoyed with the box, she screamed for Emelda to come and help her.

"I'm don't want to play outside! I'm going inside to get Maggie!"

"You can't leave the island. No one will bring you anywhere. I hate dolls! Emelda close the door. She stays outside with me. We're burning down that tree!"

When Emelda got to the door to close it, she saw in the distance Antoine coming on the quilt. She screamed, "Ophelia, LOOK over there!"

Ophelia looked up and saw this doll on a quilt coming towards her. Her hatred and fear of dolls just freaked her out. Running in the yard with Molly, she regained her balance quickly, and sobered up just as quickly. She finally lit the torch.

"Stay BACK! If you're the daddy of this one here, I will set her on fire. I will. I swear I will. Get back!"

Molly looked up and screamed, "DADDY!"

Antoine stopped in midair. "Let her go, I'm taking her and Maggie home, and you can stay and live on your island all alone. We won't bother you. Just give me my daughters!"

The Queen was crying in the tree on her quilt. Madame Plume and Madame Poulette were consoling her and crying along with her. "What can we do?" I feel so helpless right here just watching."

Marie La Vie said, "Let Antoine handle this one. He can do what he needs to do. No worry. Everything will end as it should end. We stay here."

Ophelia got so afraid of Antoine that she aimed the blazing torch at him, but when she swung the torch underhanded, it hit Molly who was standing in front of her in the front yard. Antoine and the ladies in the tree watched in horror as Molly went up in flames. It didn't take long for her to become nothing but ashes. Ophelia ran back into the house. For the first time in her life she was terrified. She terrified so many people in her life, and now she knew the feeling.

Antoine stood up on the quilt. He screamed so loud, the birds flew out of every tree there was around the island. He folded both hands into a fist and pushed hard. Huge lightning bolts shot out of both of his hands. The bolts hit the roof and the whole top of the house went flying into the sky. Then, he went after Ophelia. He knew there was nothing he could do for Molly. She was burned to ashes on the ground, and he needed to save Maggie.

When the ghost girl heard the loud boom from the roof flying away from the house she untied Maggie and took her out the back door. She was going to keep her safe in the well, but Marie La Vie didn't know this. When she saw a ghost-looking figure running with Maggie, she and the Cajun Fairies immediately left the tree and flew in the air on her magic flying quilt to get Maggie.

None of them knew anything about this place, and she wasn't taking any chances with Maggie. Molly was gone. The Queen was sobbing uncontrollably after seeing Molly being burnt, and was of no help at all.

She was inconsolable.

Madame Plume and Madame Poulette were trying to console her, but it was no use. Plume knew that Molly was burnt beyond repair. They didn't even see Marie La Vie leaving the tree to get Maggie. When Marie La Vie landed the quilt in the back yard, Maggie ran to her. She grabbed Maggie in a tight hug and told her she was safe now.

"Where you was taking Maggie?" she asked the ghost girl.

"I was inside the house. I heard everything. Ophelia is a terrible human. All humans are not like her. I untied Maggie to save her from Ophelia when I heard a loud boom. I was going to hide her in the well with me so she wouldn't hurt her."

"You did a good deed. Why you in the well, and how long have you been there?" Marie asked with kindness. She could hear Antoine was still in a rage inside of the house. She didn't know what he was doing, but there was so much noise in the house.

I don't know how long I've been in the well. I fell inside of it a long time ago, and my parents thought I was kidnapped, so they moved off the island from grief. They never heard my cries for help, so I died in the well. I wish I could go back with my mom and dad. Will Maggie go back with her mom and dad?"

"Yes she will. In a little while her mama and her daddy will see her. But first I will help you to go back to your mom and dad. Do you believe that they are in the sky? Have they crossed over?"

"Yes, I know they have crossed over. I see them. They see me. But we don't know how to meet."

"I will help you, because you helped Maggie. I will summon a white light from the sky to take you up. You go in the white light. Your mom and dad will be waiting for you." Marie smiled at her.

"Oh thank you!" The little girl was crying. Maggie never let go of Marie La Vie's dress. She held on so tight, and Acadia and Olivia were crying with the ghost girl. The fairies had a soft heart about her being reunited with her family.

With a few words from a ritual of peace and love for the dearly departed, and some sprinkles of Marie's rose water, a beautiful white light came down from the sky. The white light shined only on the ghost girl.

"Go my dear one. Go up in the white light. Your mom and dad will be there for you."

The ghost girl did as she was told and she was finally at peace. Maggie, the fairies, and Marie La Vie watched the ghost girl walk up into the white light as she blew them a kiss.

Marie put Maggie on her flying quilt, and zoomed over to Antoine. Maggie never let go of her white dress and now she was holding her by the neck. Marie told Maggie to put her face on her shoulder and to keep her eyes closed until she told her to open them. Marie La Vie could see the inside of the house from the top of the blown off roof.

Antoine had wrecked all of Ophelia's radar room and most of her house looking for Maggie. Marie yelled at Antoine to tell him that she had Maggie. He didn't hear her. He kept shooting lightning bolts inside of the house.

She flew her magic quilt to the side window. "Maggie, yell for your daddy. He will hear you."

Maggie screamed, "DADDY!"

Everything went silent for a split second. Then they heard, "MAGGIE where are you?"

"Outside daddy! Come outside. I'm with Marie La Vie. I'm okay on the magic flying quilt."

Antoine walked out on the front porch and saw Maggie. He got on his flying quilt and went over to where she was. "Oh, Maggie! You okay?"

"Yes Daddy. Marie came and get me by the well. Can we go home?"

"Molly's gone baby, but I'm glad Marie La Vie saved you!" She jumped on her daddy's flying guilt and he gave her a tight hug.

"How did you find her Marie?"

"It's a long story. I tell you later. We just say thank you to a little ghost girl, and leave it like that," she smiled.

Ophelia stepped out on the porch when she heard no more booms from the lightning bolts.

"HEY, *daddy*. I see you have your little girl. Go now and leave me alone. You wrecked my house! Look at it!"

"I wrecked your house to find my daughter and you're not bothered that YOU set my other little girl on fire, and she's gone! I have a thunder in my heart, and it feels like it's going to ROAR!"

"Antoine, you can't cross the line of ending!" Marie La Vie screamed.

"Ophelia set my daughter on fire, Marie. She crossed a line of ending! Molly is only a pile of ashes now." Antoine was furious, hurt, and sad. He had so many emotions going on at that moment. He really wanted to end the life of Ophelia right there.

"Antoine, I was watching from the tree. She saw you coming and wanted to get you, not Molly. The torch hit Molly before it could get up in the air to you." Marie had to make him understand. "Ophelia is cruel. She's a horrible human being, but you can't cross the line of ending. Not now. Things will happen to you if you do that. I don't know what things, but your life will never be the same -- NO more. Please hear me!" Marie La Vie was begging.

"Marie. Here, take Maggie."

Antoine roared again. "Then I will lock you up on your own island, Ophelia! I'll listen to Marie La Vie. She's a wise woman, but YOU, you will go nowhere. You will see no one. You will be alone. FOREVER!" Antoine shot bolts of lightning from his hands and a heavy 20-foot-tall, iron fence, began to surround the island. Each fence piece pounded into the ground with a loud BOOM.

Marie La Vie saw the three dwarf sisters leave through the back door and take off in the pirogue before they were trapped on that island with Ophelia. Ophelia was screaming, "NO, don't leave me! Stay on the island with me," but they didn't hear her and left anyway.

Marie thought they didn't want to stay with her anymore and this was their chance to leave Ophelia for good. She was right.

The fence made a loud noise as each big, 20-foot-high, heavy black iron picket fence, connected together around the island. There was just enough room between the iron pickets for her to see the water. He made sure each fence stake was tighter than the spaces at the gate of Lacey Laurel Lane, where she couldn't pass through the gate spaces. He made sure that there was no way she could dig her way out either. That fence was buried deep into the ground.

Queen Faustina, Madame Plume and Madame Poulette all kept their faces buried in their dresses, crying the whole while they heard the horrible noise of the fence wrapping around the island. They couldn't bear to look.

Marie La Vie tore a piece of her dress and whispered into Olivia's ear. She did what she said. Acadia was still on Marie's shoulder. Maggie had her head buried into Marie's white dress. She didn't want to see or hear anything.

Olivia flew on the island and began brushing up the ashes of Molly and placed them in Marie's piece of dress. It took Olivia a while to get all of the ashes into the piece of white cloth.

Suddenly, everything was quiet, and Ophelia was left alone on that island.

Antoine heard Ophelia begging, "PLEASE don't leave me here alone. I have no Quizard. I have no one to argue with. I have nothing but Cromwell, and he's dead. He's a mummy!"

Antoine got Maggie from Marie La Vie and brought her back to the Queen. When he got to the tree that Madame Plume had made, they were all so sad about Molly, but so happy Maggie was back with them. Antoine hugged the Queen and Maggie was right there in between both of them.

"Oh Sha," said Poulette, "I don't know what happened, and I think I'll leave it like that. I don't think my mind can take any more bad memories of today. We have Maggie back, and we need to go back home and move on. I'm just so sorry about Molly."

Madame Plume held onto Madame Poulette. "Marie told us that everything was going to end up the way it was supposed to, and this is what happened. You're right Poulette, we just need to go home and move forward with our lives. No looking back." They all had one last cry.

Marie La Vie was still at the fence listening to Ophelia begging to get out while the rest were getting ready to go back to the doll land. Acadia was still with Marie. Olivia was still brushing ashes into the piece of white cloth for Marie's dress.

Marie spoke to Ophelia before she left with the rest of them.

"I know it's too late for me to tell you this, but maybe you will change the way you are and rebuild your place or your way of living, so it's my duty to say this to you." Ophelia was holding on to the iron fence with both hands, her face just fitting in the space of the iron fence. She was still begging to let her out.

"Ophelia, you can't treat people the way you do and expect your life to go well. That can never happen. What you give out will always come back to you. Hatred stems from ignorance, but I swear after seeing your behavior, I do believe you were born with hatred in your heart. If you decide to change your ways and make it alone on this island, remember, peace begins inside of you."

Ophelia's face was aging as Marie La Vie was speaking to her. Her skin was flabby and her face looked like ice cream melting down on the cone.

"The time of 3:33 pm had nothing to do with me getting a new Quizard to keep me beautiful, did it?"

"Oh Mon Gris-Gris. That's all you have to say. You have no

concern for anyone or anything except for yourself and the way you look. This is why you needed this Quizard? To make yourself beautiful?" Marie shook her head and spread some of her rose water on Ophelia. Not that it would do any good, but this is what Marie knew she had to do.

"Ophelia, you will never be beautiful, because beauty lives inside you. You don't have that."

Marie took her quilt, turned it around quickly and went to the tree with everyone else. They were all waiting for her to come back to the tree to leave together.

Madame Plume said, "I don't know about any of you, but I'm whipped to a frazzle."

No one else said a word, so Plume sat quietly next to Madame Poulette. Maggie stayed sitting on the Queen's lap. Marie told Antoine that she was done with that horrible place and she never wanted to see it again. Antoine led the way back to the Doll Land of Sha Bebe.

As they all were leaving the big tree to go back to the doll land, they heard a loud boom! They looked back and saw Olivia flying faster than they ever saw a fairy fly before.

"Wait for me! The old house just blew up." She was holding the white cloth with Molly's ashes.

Ophelia's name was never mentioned again.

Chapter 10

A Farewell for Molly

When the quilts landed on the braided rug road, one of the sugar mill ladies rang the dinner bell on the porch and everyone came running out of their homes to cheer their return. All you could hear were cheers of *'YAY, they're home'* coming for everyone. Hugs were going around to everyone. Miss Betty Lou got the 100 boys and girls in line after they had their happy moment. The sugar mill ladies were standing by. The rest of the Cajun Fairies hovered overhead. Everyone was waiting to see Princess Maggie and Princess Molly again.

Marie La Vie stepped off of her quilt first. Antoine helped Queen Faustina off of her quilt with Princess Maggie in her arms. Madame Plume and Madame Poulette got off of the quilts last. Antoine looked at his Queen with sad eyes and asked her if she wanted to speak to everyone. She couldn't. Her heart was broken. She wanted him to tell the family about Molly. So he began to speak.

"I want to tell everyone that we have some bad news about what happened today. We found the *humans* who took Maggie and Molly away from us, but the house had a very *mean human* living there, and …. There was a fire. We brought Maggie home."

Princess Maggie and Queen Faustina walked up to Antoine and stood by his side. Everyone cheered when they saw Princess Maggie. Antoine looked at Queen Faustina and didn't know what to say. His heart was broken, and he couldn't speak another word.

Princess Maggie took a step forward to speak. Everyone stood still.

"I'm here today because Molly was born to save me. There was a fire at the house we were in and Molly was burned in the fire. Molly's not here anymore." She bowed her head down.

Everyone gasped, and began to cry.

"No. Listen to me," pleaded Princess Maggie. "All of you don't need to feel sad. Molly was an angel sent here just for me. She knew before she was born she had to come here to save me, so she came here on her own. I'm a Quizard who was destined to be here with my Queen Mama and my Wizard Daddy. This is how it was meant to be. I will always be grateful to Molly. We will always remember Molly. But she told me not to be sad. Sha is an angel."

"So I didn't POP Molly to life. I knew I didn't do that. Right, Maggie?" Madame Plume was so relieved that her wand was still in working order.

"Madame Plume, no you didn't pop Molly to life, but you did POP me to life. Molly came to the doll land on her own, through your wand. She told me that she had to come here or I would have burned in the fire. She came here to protect me, because I'm a rare Quizard. I need a magic key that is here. She told me she would be okay and not to worry or be sad about her because she's an angel." Molly bowed her head.

Queen Faustina turned to Marie La Vie, "I didn't know she knew about a magic key. I'm a little surprised about that."

"Oh yes, she knows that and much more." Marie smiled with her hands clasped together as usual.

Princess Maggie continued, "I have a blue heart. All of you have a pink heart. There is a magic key in this land that will light my heart, but I think my time ended to turn the key to get my magic. If this happened, I'm the same as all of you, except I'm blue," she shrugged her shoulders "All I have is a blue heart full of love for all of you with no magic."

She ran to Antoine as everyone applauded.

"Oh, your mama and I love you very much. Makes us no difference if your blue heart lights up or not. You have a home and a family here in the doll land of Sha Bebe with everything you will ever need." She gave her daddy a big hug and then went to her mama and hugged her.

"Yes, my Princess. All you will ever need is here in the doll land. You won't need to worry about anything ever again. Just be happy."

"Come and give Aunt Plume a big hug!"

Princess Maggie stayed with her mama. "Your feathers tickle me," she giggled.

"Then, I will make all of my dresses with soft feathers from now on." Plume went to Faustina and Maggie jumped in her arms. "I know you love your Aunt Plume. I will make you many pretty dresses. You will love it here with all of the other boys and girls."

"I have another announcement to make. Tomorrow morning, we will have a memorial for Molly, because now we know Maggie would not be here if Molly had not entered the land. Faustina and I will think of what we will do tonight. At sunrise, everyone be dressed and at the statues of Jacque and Evangeline." He bowed his head. "Thank you"

Olivia interrupted, "I have the ashes of Molly in here."

"Oh! How did you do this? For the love of Sha Bebe, Marie, this is a piece of your dress!"

Queen Faustina was crushed but so pleased to have the ashes of Molly.

"Yes, I sent Olivia to pick up her ashes so she would not stay on the other side of that fence. It didn't feel right. I tore the apron of my dress. Olivia flew to the ashes and brushed them into my piece of dress."

Faustina was holding the cloth of ashes. Stunned. Then all of a sudden, she spoke. "Tonight Antoine will make Molly a gold box. Our little angel's ashes will be placed in that gold box and placed at the statues tomorrow morning. Be there at sunrise. This is how we will have the memorial. I am ever so grateful that we do have Molly back home too. Thank you Marie and Olivia." She bowed to them. They returned the bow.

Poulette applauded, softly. Everyone else joined in with a soft applaud of approval.

"Okay!" the Queen continued, after taking a deep breath, "I've been told that everyone has had their suppertime, so after we go and eat our supper, we'll all get ready for bed. The land is back to normal," she smiled, while still holding Maggie. This has been a very stressful day for all of us, and we all need rest. Tomorrow is a new day, and we shall celebrate. We will not mourn."

Everyone agreed.

On the way to supper, Queen Faustina asked Marie, "Everything is back to normal, right?"

"As far as I know, everything is very good." Marie winked.

Chapter 11

The Magic Key

The next morning was a beautiful day. The sun rose brightly, the roosters were crowing, and the smell of honey suckle filled the air. Everyone was gathered at the statues of Jacque and Evangeline for the memorial of Princess Molly. After the memorial, they would all gather in the dining room for an early lunch.

"Poulette, let's do *the Dance of the Flying Plates* for Maggie at brunch. Is that okay with you? I think she would like to see that. Last night at suppertime wasn't a good time to do it." The Queen was smiling.

"Oh, yes! I'll go quickly and tell the sugar mill ladies that we'll have a slight change in plans. Ah Sha, Princess Maggie will love that. I'll be right back."

"Take your time. Nothing is promised to us as each minute goes by. Take your time."

When Poulette returned to tell the Queen that she and the sugar mill ladies were ready for this festive brunch, she noticed that Princess Maggie stayed very close to Queen Faustina, holding on to her dress. The three of them walked over to the statues of Jacque and Evangeline.

Beings that none of them in the doll land had ever performed a memorial before, except Marie La Vie, or even been to one for that matter, they all followed her lead. In the city she had gone to many

Jazz funerals, and spoke at many ceremonies. She asked everyone to gather together in front of the statues.

Queen Faustina, Princess Maggie, Wizard Antoine, Madame Plume, Madame Poulette, Marie La Vie, Miss Betty Lou with the 100 boys and girls, sixteen sugar mill ladies, Acadia and Olivia with 20 other Cajun Fairies hovering overhead…. Everyone was there. Even a few Cajun Angels were watching from above.

"Antoine, do you have the ashes of Princess Molly?"

"Yes, I do." He walked up to the statues and placed the shiny gold box that he made with his own two hands in the middle of the both statues.

Princess Maggie was still holding on to the Queen's dress.

Marie La Vie stepped in front of the statues and said her words of wisdom for Princess Molly. She said thank you, and then praised Princess Molly for her part in saving Princess Maggie from all harm. Her bravery would never be forgotten. She would forever be a hero to everyone in the doll land of Sha Bebe. The ceremony was beautifully done.

When Marie La Vie finished her gracious sermon, she sprinkled rose water on the gold box. After the sprinkling, she raised her two arms up in a final praise of thanks and closed her eyes as she bowed her head and asked for a moment of silence. At that moment,

Marie La Vie heard everyone's voices moaning, and there were a few who gasped. There was no silence. When she opened her eyes, there in front of her were the spirits of Jacque and Evangeline. She stepped back with Antoine and Queen Faustina.

"Did you call my parents here, Marie?"

"No Antoine! I did not. They are here on their own."

They spoke:

"Greetings my son. We're here with a message for you and your Queen." Jacque was like a shining light in front of the stone wall.

"Greetings my children," repeated Evangeline. "It's a blessing to see my children Antoine and Plume, and my granddaughter Princess Maggie."

Their voices were like echoes. They spoke in a rhyme at the same time:

"Something as precious as a child, is with you inside forever.

A greater love ... there can never be found.... Ever.

Plume and Antoine were connected together;

sister and brother.

Wait for the key, there will be another."

When Evangeline finished her words, both of them stopped

glowing against the stone wall, and they disappeared. There was only the stone wall with the statues.

Jacque and Evangeline appeared at the statues.

"What do you think that meant?" asked Plume.

Everyone was silent.

"I have no idea," said Antoine. "Sister and brother connected, and wait for a key?"

Queen Faustina was thinking out loud. "It has to mean something. Why would they appear at Molly's memorial?"

"I don't know," said Marie La Vie. "They did not mention Princess Molly, only Princess Maggie."

The boys and girls didn't know what to think of all of this, so Queen Faustina explained that they just wanted to say goodbye to Molly. Everything was just fine. They were satisfied with that explanation.

"So what do we do now?" Madame Poulette asked. "Go to our brunch, or stay here to see if they will return. I'm stumped about what the words meant."

"So am I, Poulette. What do we do? Their appearance made me feel so joyful inside. Then, to hear our mama say, 'our children' to me and Antoine one more time. Oh!" Plume fanned herself with her hands. Her heart was overjoyed.

They all stood there in silence for a few minutes and then Plume began picking up the doorknob chimes that were left on the ground when they were all looking for the magic key the night the girls were abducted. It was too late to do the Blue Chant, and the beautiful ceremony was over. But why did Jacque and Evangeline appear?

With each doorknob chime Madame Plume picked up, she was talking to herself and wondering what the words meant. As she picked up each chime, she put the key into the keyhole. When she got to the third chime and tuned the key, a camouflage blanket slowly came floating down to the ground. On the blanket was another blue doll.

No one said a word. Plume was still talking about the rhyme and picking up the doorknob chimes.

"Plume, look!" said Madame Poulette as she nudged her in the side.

"Look at what? Someone needs to pick up the chimes and save them. I don't know what will happen next now that Marie said we have a magic key in the land on one of these doorknobs. It's still here, you know."

"No, Plume. Look up!"

"I didn't do that! I don't have my wand. I was picking up the doorknob chimes and just talking to myself. I didn't have anything at all to do with this one, Antoine!"

The Queen and Antoine were stunned to see another blue doll. But the flying blanket looked like some kind of netting.

"Chimes!" Madame Plume spoke up. "These are the chimes with the keys! But who is the blue doll, and *what are those clothes?*

Camouflage netting?" Her face made a grimace.

"I don't know. Your guess is as good as mine," said Madame Poulette. I didn't have anything to do with making a camouflage blanket." She stepped back.

"Who are you?" asked the Queen.

"This doll is the answer to the riddle," said Marie. "And, she is holding the magic key in her hand!"

"I *knew* that magic key wasn't in that pile," whispered the Queen.

"Well, I thought I had the magic key here in the pile of doorknob chimes, Marie. Look at all of these keys." Madame Plume was very confused.

The camouflage blanket was still floating down.

"Makes no difference how many keys in the land. That key is the magic key."

"Then, where is the doorknob chime?"

"In the pile," Marie answered. "Let's watch and see what happens."

The camouflage blanket landed on the ground.

"Oh my goodness." Madame Plume looked in amazement at Antoine and Faustina. "Who is she? How did she get here, *and what is she wearing*? For a second, I thought she was a boy."

Everyone could see the new blue doll well on the ground. She did have clothes on that was fit for a boy doll. \

Princess Maggie ran to the new blue doll and said, "Kira, I've been waiting for you. Molly told me you would be coming with me, but I didn't know how you would get here or when!" They embraced. Princess Kira gave the magic key to Princess Maggie. She walked to the pile of doorknob chimes and picked one. "This is the right doorknob for the magic key." Maggie smiled and gave it to Antoine.

Kira with the Magic Key

Silence. Complete silence. Only Marie La Vie had a big grin on her face.

Madame Poulette broke the silence once again. "Awe Sha, another Princess has entered the doll land of Sha Bebe. Now, we have real twin Quizards in the doll land of Sha Bebe!"

"Hi. I'm Maggie's real twin sister. I couldn't enter when she did. It wasn't my time to enter the doll land."

"Are you our Princess, too?"

"Yes, I am. I'm all yours. Ta Da! And, I'm glad to be here." Kira slapped her camouflage netting that she flew in on over her shoulder. It wasn't a blanket or a quilt. It was camouflage netting.

The Queen and the Wizard were confused and trying to understand how a doll entered the doll land without the magic wand of Madame Plume. "No magic wand, Marie?"

"No wand is needed for the Quizard. Only the presences of a magic key, a Queen and a Wizard. Everything was right for the Quizard to be born here. Kira is yours!" said Marie La Vie with a huge smile on her face.

"Princess Maggie told me that my wand brought her in the doll land. Is this true, or did she want to make me feel good?

"Yes it is true. The Quizard comes through anyway they find where there is a magic key, a Queen, and a Wizard. Princess Maggie came through your wand. Princess Kira came when you put a key in the door chime." Marie explained.

"Antoine, I did bring both of them here! Did you hear Marie?"

"Yes I did. You are the best doll maker ever...And the best aunt."

"Oh thank you, Antoine!" She actually blushed.

"For the love of Sha Bebe. Twin Quizards. Antoine, we have twin Quizards!"

"I see that." Antoine's smile was like gold as he watched them playing around the statues, but Princess Kira was a little rougher than Princess Maggie.

Marie's feet stayed planted firmly on the ground, her hands placed inside each other. "Kira is the answer to the rhyme of Evangeline when she said 'connected as sister and brother, wait for the key, there will be another'. I am amazed! Truly amazed."

"I thought she was a boy with those clothes, but look at her long eyelashes. She's beautiful, and I'm her aunt. Well, if that don't beat all," Madame Plume laughed. "What an odd mixtures of fabrics though. Khaki and velvet with camouflage. Tomorrow I'll make her some girly clothes fit for a Princess."

"She's good dressed like that, Plume. She may be a little bit of a tom boy, but that's fine. Maggie is a girly girl. Let them be who they are," Antoine said to Plume.

"Okay, if you say so. You're her daddy."

"Yes I am. A very proud daddy."

Princess Maggie and Princess Kira were still playing, and it became more obvious as they watched them that Kira was much rougher than Maggie, but she was the cutest little blue doll ever.

"Don't worry about Kira's clothes, Plume," said the Queen. "If she's a tom boy, that's who she is. Nothing wrong with that at all."

"Oh no, Faustina. I'm not worried about that," she turned her head to Madame Poulette and made a grimace. "I will love her just the way she is, and we'll all just let her be who she is."

Madame Plume turned to Poulette and whispered, "Have you ever seen any of my dolls dressed like that? I'll have her dressed like a Princess by tomorrow."

"Maybe she likes dressing like this. Maybe she is a tom boy. Did you ever think about that, Plume?"

Madame Plume just stood there and wondered. "Well, not everyone loves feathers and frills. You're right Poulette. They are the twin Princesses of this land, woven so tightly together by thought that they were both weaved into one long piece of fabric. It's just that the fabrics on Kira don't match." She laughed.

With those words, Madame Plume accepted that a tom boy may be roaming the doll land. It really made her no difference. They were her family. Twin nieces.

Everyone was still standing at the statues adoring both blue dolls. Princess Maggie and Princess Kira came running to their mama and daddy. Princess Kira jumped on Wizard Antoine. Princess Maggie jumped on Queen Faustina.

"Well, if this is not a perfect ending to a horrible event, I don't know what is," said Madame Plume. "One Quizard for each of you. The doll land is very secure, and they will be safe here for all eternity. Antoine, where will we put the chime and the magic key? It can't go back up in the big oak tree. Remember the legend of every 50 years? Marie wants both of them hidden very well."

"Oh, I'll make sure this doorknob chime and this key are in a safe place. Not to worry about that."

"I have a suggestion," said Madame Poulette. "Princess Kira just entered the land, so let's do the Blue Chant and the Turning of the Magic Key before we go to our festive brunch. We don't want to take any chances again with *human* time. Do we?"

"Great idea!" The Queen clapped her hands together. "No more *time* for us. Everyone stay where you are, and Marie La Vie will do the honors of saying The Blue Chant. Soon we will see what magical powers our Princess Kira possesses."

Marie La Vie set herself up at the shrine of Jacque and Evangeline. Madame Plume handed her the magical doorknob key chime. While Queen Faustina held Maggie, she and Antoine each held the hand of Princess Kira.

Marie La Vie began turning the magic key while saying The Blue Chant.

"With this key for our Quizard, we turn it to the left,
We unleash the magic of hope and love to be blessed,
Inside the blue heart, we light the light for our child,
Let the magic be for good and let it run wild."

Immediately you could see Princess Kira's blue heart light up through her clothes. It shined as bright as the sun. The blue light radiated outward like a flashlight. Everyone was so excited, but they kept silent. They didn't know what to do or what would happen.

Marie La Vie smiled and assured everyone that this is how everything was supposed to be. She turned to look at Princess Maggie, and she saw a little glimmer of a blue light coming out from her dress. Not as bright as the light shining from Princess Kira, but there was a blue light!

"Faustina, look at Princess Maggie."

When Faustina held her up, she saw the blue light. "For the love of Sha Bebe! Is Maggie a Quizard with magical powers too?"

Antoine was looking at both of them with the same amazement as Queen Faustina. "Yep, I'm sure she is. Her blue light … lit up!" His deep jovial laugh could be head all over the land.

When Marie La Vie applauded with a cheer saying, "Oh Mon Gris-Gris! We DO have two Quizards," everyone else cheered with her.

The ovation was spectacular. The Bebe Land Band played music. The sugar mill ladies came running out. It was past brunch. After they saw what happened with another Quizard, they cheered and went to make more food.

"What a festive occasion for the doll land of Sha Bebe. Let's make them a cake!" The sugar mill ladies quickly ran inside and began baking a royal cake for the two Princesses.

Princess Kira and Princess Maggie stood side by side. Maggie asked, "Do you already know what magical power was bestowed upon you?"

"Yes, I have the gift of cloaking. My camouflage cape can make me invisible." She took her cape and put it over her head, and she became invisible. She let the cape drop down and she reappeared.

"I was told I had the gift of enchantment. I can turn objects and humans into anything I want." Maggie saw a rock on the ground, she tilted her head forward and the rock became a bird. She let it fly away.

Everyone cheered, but the Queen and Antoine were just a little anxious about how this would work out in the doll land. They would need to be taught when and how to use their magic. They both applauded Maggie and Kira and told them how proud they were of them. After the cheering, the Queen announced that an extra special lunch was being served with extra dessert for everyone.

Madame Plume said, "WELL, this should be a LOT of fun. Princess Kira, a girl who dresses like a boy can become invisible, and the regal looking Princess Maggie can turn objects and *humans* into anything she wants. HA. LOADS of fun. I can see it all now. He-he!"

Princess Maggie and Princess Kira walked along the braided rug road for the first time to the kitchen with the rest of the dolls. The Queen followed everyone to Madame Poulette's kitchen where they all would sit for what was now lunch. The kitchen was filled with lots of food and desserts as well. In the middle of the room was a three tier cake to welcome the Princesses to the doll land of Sha Bebe.

While walking to the kitchen, Queen Faustina asked Marie La Vie, "I thought we had 24 *human* hours for a Quizard to get their magic. What happened with that?"

"Oh, you know how *human* time is." She rolled her eyes. "Sometimes legends are measured by our time, and sometimes it is measured by *human* time." She winked. "One never knows. One must make their own waves and not worry about the splashes others are making in the bayou." Marie La Vie laughed.

Meanwhile, Antoine went to the statue of his parents, and with the lightning bolts from his hands, he popped a deep hole in the ground between the statues. He made a strong box of pink stones. He placed the magic doorknob chime with the magic key into the box and placed it deep inside the hole in between each statue. When he thanked his parents for their appearance, a small white light shined from each statue's heart for a few seconds.

"Thank you! I don't know how long our lives will last here in the doll land, so until we become spirits like you, please guard this box well. I love you both and good bye for now."

He bowed. Antoine left to catch up with the rest to eat their festive meal.

"Wait for me. I don't want to miss Maggie and Kira watching the Dance of the Flying plates." Antoine laughed out loud.

No one ever heard Antoine laugh this loud. His laugh was as jovial as Santa. And to make things even sweeter, they were in the human month of December.

The Doll Land of Sha Bebe was indeed a magical place to be.

The Dance of the Flying Plates
in
Madame Poulette's Dining Room

Princess Maggie and Princess Kira had so much fun watching the magic of the flying plates dancing through the air. The food stayed on the plates and not one drop of any food ever spilled to the floor or on the table.

Awe Sha. They will be in for so much more fun with all of the magic in The doll Land of Sha Bebe.

The Bebe Land Band played music all day and everyone ate, danced, and enjoyed this day more than the wedding day.

At the end of the day, Queen Faustina and Wizard Antoine flew into the sky on a magic quilt ride for their honeymoon in the city of New Orleans, as Madame Plume suggested. As both of them toured the city, they agreed that the doll land of Sha Bebe was so much more peaceful than human land. Oh yea, so much more peaceful. They saw how they looked to each other ...... As humans.

In the doll land, they deal with issues that come up. The dolls are a close knit family unit. When something breaks, they fix it and move on. When they disagree, they make up and move on. When trouble arrives, they get together as a family, get rid of the trouble, and move on. Moving on is a big lesson in the doll land of Sha Bebe. It's the only way that the land stayed alive since the beginning of time.

There is that word again. *TIME.*

The End

You think so, Sha?

The Sugar Mill Ladies Waving to the Princesses

Now --- it's The End.

It's all Bayou Chic, Sha.

In loving memory Linda who was like a sister to me.

Rest in Peace Dada 10-12-15

Remembering --Here we stand with our first dolls.

About the Author

Mary Lynn Hebert Plaisance has been writing her stories about the doll land of Sha Bebe since 2004. The dolls came first. Then the stories evolved with each character she created. She made her first doll in 1991 and received a copyright for the Sha Bebe Dolls in 1992. When her four sons left the family home to live on their own, as it happens with every family, her dolls filled her empty nest syndrome in a small way. She was able to build characters, and "take care" of her dolls the way she took care of her sons. She named each doll she made. The dolls filled a void in her heart.

In 2001 she thought about writing the first short story for her special dolls who would live in the sugar cane fields of Louisiana. Sugar cane fields surrounded her home all of her life, so why not have the dolls living in the fields. Her grandpa told her that all of the good dolls come from the sugar cane fields. From there the story telling grew.

She began creating a doll land, and this was the beginning of her endless fairytale stories. She will continue to write stories as long as an adventure enters her mind. She now calls her books, *"The Chronicles of Sha Bebe"*.

You can connect with Mary Lynn on Facebook or on Twitter.

---

facebook.com/Mary.Lynn.H.Plaisance/

twitter.com/CajunDollHouse

My Cajun Fairies Olivia and Acadia

Google

Mary Lynn Hebert Plaisance

Beb's Cajun Doll House

Thank you. Enjoy Every Day. Enjoy Sha Bebe

You can purchase all Mary Lynn's books on Amazon.com

Thank you.

Stay tuned. ☺

Jolie and Beau, until we meet again.

****

Made in the USA
Charleston, SC
20 December 2015